**prose and cons**
**len barry**

This book is partly a work of fiction and partly memoir in the forms of short stories (fantasy, sci-fi, post-dystopia, and historical fiction), plus poetry, opinion, and lyrics of the author.



For permissions, write:
blueroombooks@outlook.com
Subject: Prose and Cons

Cover design, interior layout, and edit: Angela K. Durden

Executive Editor: Tom Whitfield

Photo credits with photos, with certain exceptions, are to be understood as from the author's personal archives.

Some illustrations are part of the CorelDraw licensed package.

EAN13/ISBN 978-1-950729-06-7

PROS AND CONS
LEN BARRY
BLUEROOMBOOKS.COM

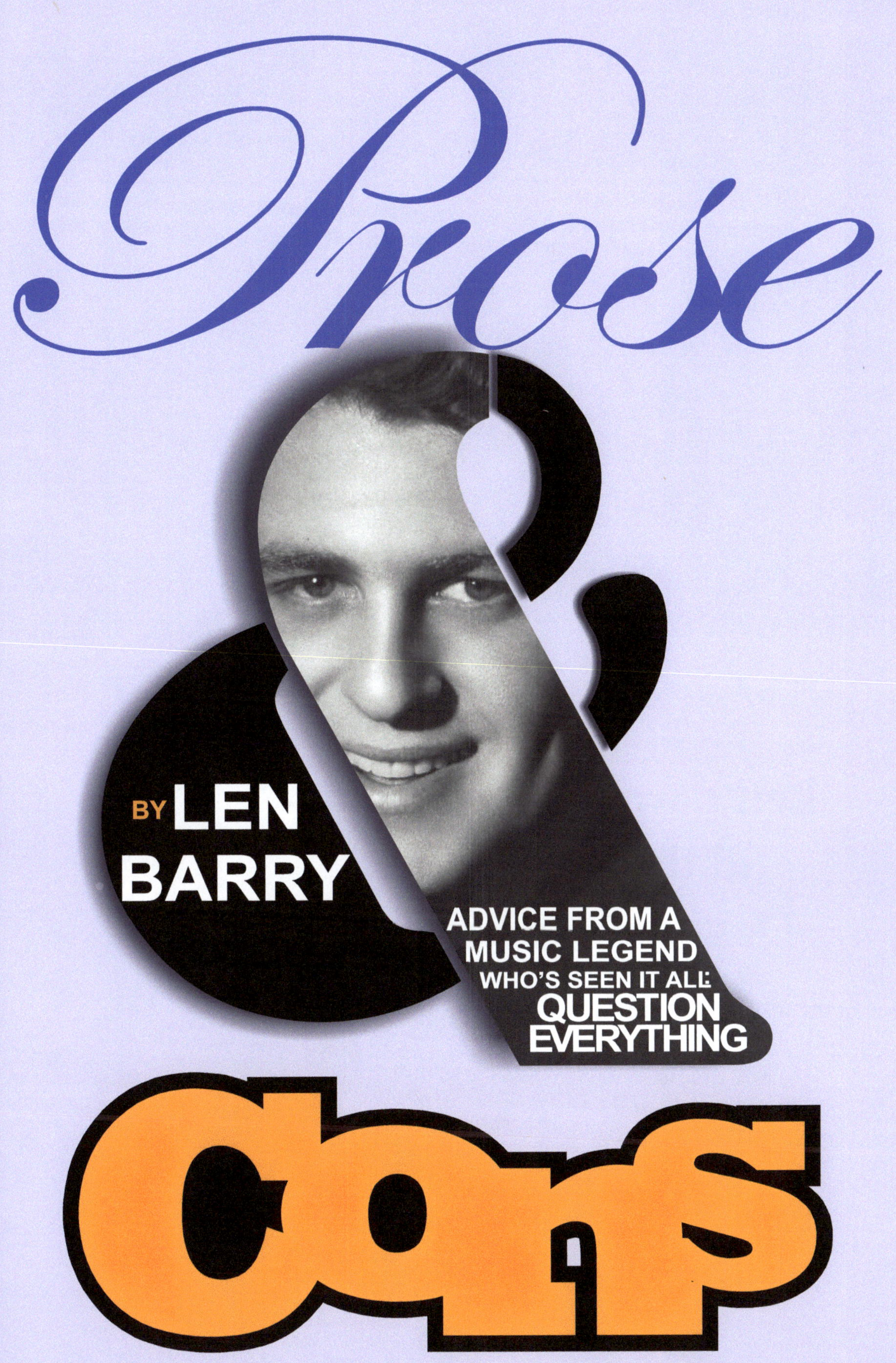
Prose
&
BY LEN BARRY
ADVICE FROM A MUSIC LEGEND WHO'S SEEN IT ALL: QUESTION EVERYTHING
Cons

**Len Barry and the Dovells**

**Above: in the movie "Don't Knock the Twist", and below: 1959 publicity photo (Author, top center)**

## A NOTE FROM THE PUBLISHER

As you read these words, people around the world are being entertained by Len Barry's music — and will continue to be for decades more to come. Chronicling a career spanning eight decades would take volumes to simply list his accomplishments as a singer, songwriter, and producer.

Isn't that the way legends roll, though? Maybe we'll take on that project another time because this book is not about Len from another's standpoint — something we believe he would find boring. Instead, *Prose and Cons* is part oil on the roiled waters of social justice, part fire in the belly of true civil rights struggles, and part autobiography of a man who has lived through it all. As he tells you to do, he follows his own advice: Question everything.

That's why we chose to publish this book, a book only an independent publisher could appreciate because we ourselves find the beaten path uninteresting and tedious. That Len Barry entrusted us with this project is something we will always value.

We are proud to present this facet of Len. In some ways it's the rest of the story of *Black-Like-Me,* he and his son Spencer's 2008 novel about a white brother and sister growing up in the 'hood.

Len has never been one to rest on past laurels because he's so busy with what is left to do. The man's mind never stops as ideas roll out like visionary tsunamis. For those who know his music but not the man from whence it sprung, we would be remiss if we didn't, at least briefly, recap only a few highlights from his career.

Before the British invasion by the Beatles and others, Len was lead singer of The Dovells, a legendary Doo Wop group from West Philly in the early 1960s that led the American invasion of Britain with such hits as *Bristol Stomp* and *You Can't Sit Down*. His solo act included several hits; *1-2-3* peaked at #2 on the Billboard chart in November 1965. Folks already knew his voice and, at 17 when he was invited by James Brown to tour with him, those same folks were surprised to hear that funkaliciousness coming from a young white boy.

A star in the United Kingdom as well as the United States, he appeared on iconic TV series including American Bandstand, Shindig, Hullabaloo, and Top of the Pops. Len put together a studio group called The Electric Indian for a brilliant 1969 instrumental called *Keem-O-Sabe* that reached #16 on Billboard. He was a major draw on tour for many years with Sam Cooke and dozens of other major acts, and performed often at The Apollo, Royal, Howard, and Regal theaters, and in Watts.

And that's just for starters.

But time passes. People get older. And as naturally as night follows day, time in the public eye declines. Len knows this is the natural order but has never stopped performing, writing, producing, and — more importantly to him — speaking up, sharing his experiences, caring about people, and showing that care by being a force for good wherever he stands.

*Prose and Cons* is performance art in print, a visual representation of the harmony and discord, the consensus, compromise, and conflict of a soul always in tune and in step with Truth – a truth that bona fide creativity always tells…even if those closest to him could not comprehend it at the time and often misunderstood it.

Blue Room Books | October 2020

No. 1060 Week ending May 8, 1967

WORLD'S LARGEST CIRCULATION OF ANY MUSIC PAPER

**ELVIS** surprise for bride

# MONKEE PETER

Exclusive revelations PLUS new pictures

**WALKER BROS SPLIT SHOCK**

**TOP POP NEWS**

Mama's & Papa's mystery • Meet the TURTLES

**Paul: 'Steve's not me'**

No. 1 SANDIE SHAW'S PUPPET ON A STRING on PYE 7N 17272 ★ MERTENS BROS. STYLE on CBS 2730

No. 4 The MAMA'S and the PAPA'S DEDICATED TO THE ONE I LOVE on RCA 1576

K.P.M., 21 DENMARK STREET, W.C.2 TEM 3856

# Len Barry makes it easy as "1·2·3"

**with his first RCA VICTOR single–**

**THE MOVING FINGER WRITES**

**c/w Our love**

**RCA 1588**

**If it's happening...it's here!**

RCA Victor Records product of The Decca Record Company Limited Decca House Albert Embankment London SE1

This collection of various poems and stories is entitled "Prose and Cons".

But do not be misled.

Many times you will find both in each. Positives in dominant negatives and, of course, vice versa.

I have chosen the written word because it is what I do best, most clearly.

Robert Kennedy said —
"Some men see things as they are and ask *why*. I dream of things that never were and ask *why not*."

Well, hey, I don't need to see either. I do not need to see squat. I feel things! I feel things first and so damn deeply that they eventually manifest into pictures.

Technicolor.
Cinemascopic.
Three-D pictures.

But prior to those pictures, there are visions. Yes, chronologically it's

Feelings.
Visions.
Photos.

The final pictures are never as wonderful as the visions that are only, in transference, even remotely as exulting as the initial, animalistically raw-gut feelings. These hallowed feelings also, simultaneously, gut shoot the mind. You see, the brain is the name of the game!

Life, the precious gift of life, takes place, is lived in the mind. The body is merely the infantry of the mind's hierarchy. The arms, legs, and other appendages, including even the most-prized fingers, are its lowly foot soldiers.

This is, unlike most of my resolutions, absolute truth.

Just ask Stephen Hawking, whose infantry was functionless. Or Stevie Wonder, whose foot soldiers fight for life on a blind, black battlefield.

So, welcome to my feelings and truths I presume you will not always share. Indeed, it would be disappointing to both of us if, in essence, you did.

L-R: Dave White, Len, John Madera

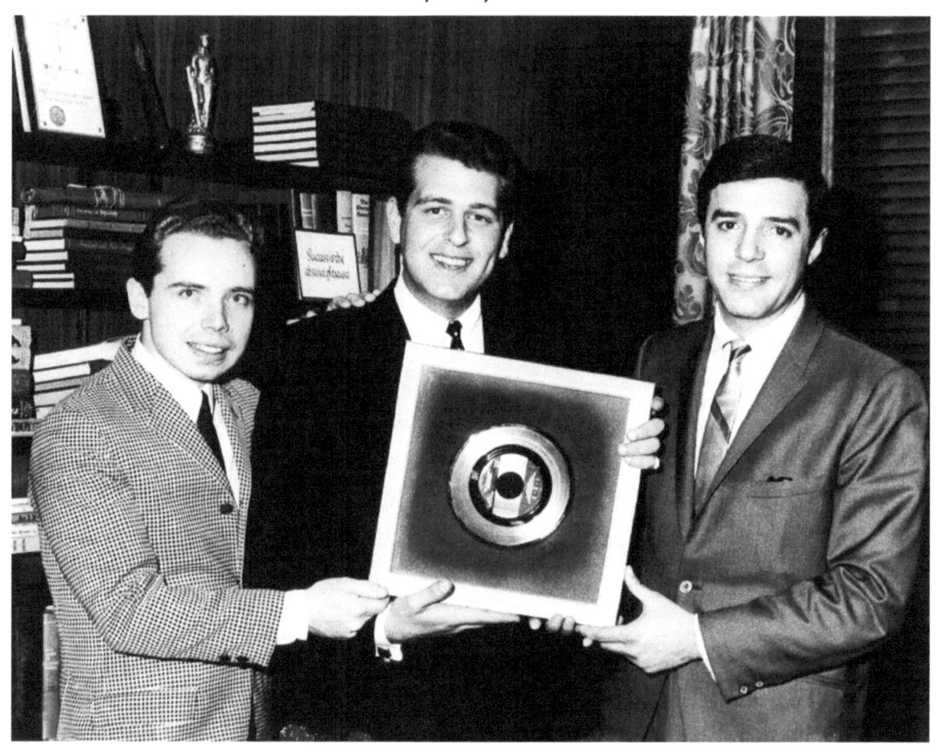

L-R: DJ Charlie Brown (WKIX Raleigh), Len, and DJ Tommy Walker.

# Intro

my first love

*my first love was a "sista"*
*I met way back in school*
*the first time that I kissed her*
*I though that we was kool*

*then they started staring*
*with fire in their eyes*
*hatred raging, glaring*
*to my naïve surprise*

*my first love was a "sista"*
*with soft brown, silky skin*
*dimple in each cheek*
*and a cleft set in her chin*

*her eyes were black as night*
*her teeth were white as snow*
*her smile seemed to follow me*
*wherever I would go*

*I remember feeling*
*eyes upon my back*
*while walkin' hand in hand*
*one white, the other black*

*her mother didn't like me*
*her dad hated my guts*
*eventually we let it get*
*between the two of us*

*she wound up with a "brotha"*
*I wound up all alone*
*I never found another*
*I loved down to the bone*

*my first love was a "sista"*
*and though the years have passed*
*every day I miss her*
*'cause my first love was my last*

James

Caught a plane for Macon
Where I'd never been before
Then drove Tobacco Road
to join **The James Brown Tour**
I was just seventeen — dumbass kid
But I could not believe how those people lived

I looked at windows without screens
in tattered, shattered shacks
And the hopeless broken dreams of
old black folks looking back
As the young 'uns played out front,
I could hear 'em laugh
Shoeless, barefoot runts that ain't never had a chance
Kids who'd never know
The wonders of life
Men made outta snow
And skates on ice
It's when I became aware all lives ain't equal
And when I learned to care 'n' share the pain of other people
The tour began that night
In ol' Magnolia Gardens
The whole town came to life
Macon came to party
Opened the show — the only white act
Ev'ry face in the place was Southern Baptist Black
But when we was done — ev'rybody clapped
Got no standin' O — but Mama ain't had no fool
Long as they liked the show — everything was cool
Next came Ben E. King — Man that dude could sing
Raspin' "darlin' darlin'" — there's a rose in "Spanish Harlem"
Then came The Crystals — pretty black New York Devils
Opened wid "Doo-Ron-Ron" — closed wid "He's a Rebel"
Then came Freda Payne — singin' "Band of Gold"
Sista's claim to fame — Ice Princess a soul

Then the MC shouted as the audience grew louder
The man who gave you these "Try Me" and "Please, Please, Please"
"Prisoner of Love", "Night Train", "Lost Someone"
Band was in a frenzy
Drumroll — extended
The "Godfather of Soul" — he hollered
But James ain't hit da stage
First the dancin' girls came
The Brownies was their name
Them came the Famous Flames
Lloyd — Bennett — Bird
Then a roar was heard
And out on stage he came
Master dancer James
King of Southern Soul
Dressed head-to-toe in gold
Without a doubt the greatest
Doin' his famous Mashed Potatoes
All across the stage
Dancin' on one leg
Then when he grabbed the mic
He groaned and owned the night
He opened with "Try Me"
With the Flames in harmony
then one after another
He played the "done-wrong" lover
From a grav'ly raspy throat
Came ev'ry perfect note
He sung "Prisoner of Love"
The ladies ate it up
He sung "Lost Someone"
Then as he came — he was gone
He done sung all his songs
I checked out ev'ry show
I watched his legend grow
A king all dressed in gold
The Godfather of Soul
The epitome of fame
Simply known as

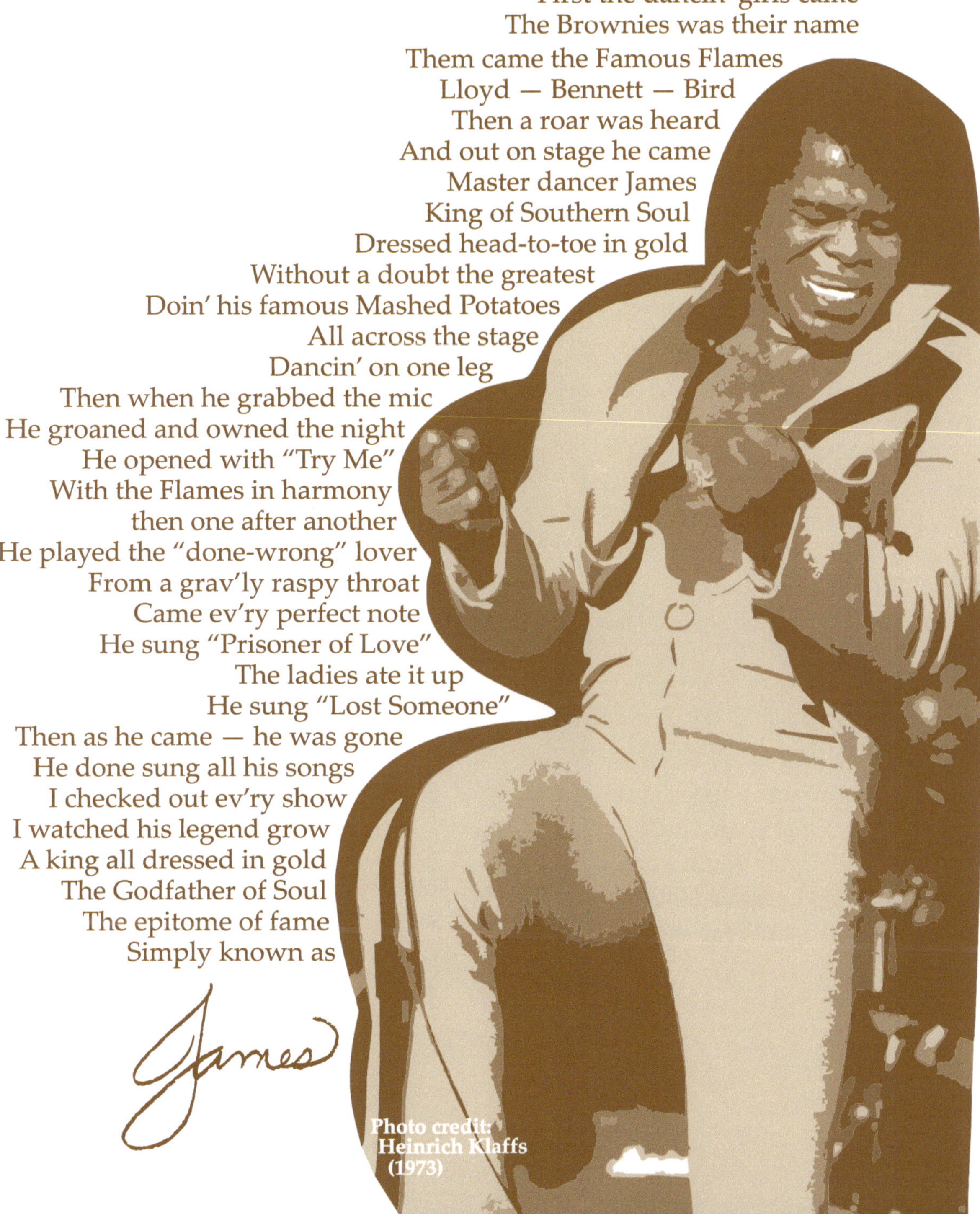


Photo credit:
Heinrich Klaffs
(1973)

# EBONY and JET

My mother came from Ukraine
My dad's from Stalingrad
Ain't an ounce o' pigment in 'em
Dat's what drives me mad

My bloodline's white as ice
So it's strange as strange kin get
Dat I done lived my whole life
in *Ebony* and *Jet*

All my friends is brothers
The chicks I hit be black
Weird as it seems, believe me
Dat's just where I'm at

R&B's my music
Since I been a kid
Tina, James, and Rufus
Funk is how I live

BET is constantly
On my TV set
All aboard the Soul Train
*Ebony* and *Jet*

*Ebony* and *Jet*
black as white kin get
The whole world knows
I'm juxtaposed
in *Ebony* and *Jet*

Why am I where I'm at
I do not know why yet
My skin is white,
my soul is black
as *Ebony* and *Jet*

We've read it hundreds of times. We've said it so many ways.
Recited it first in our nursery rhymes and all of the great Shakespeare plays.
Sometimes it comes in a song DJs on the radio play.
Eventually we all sing right along, cuz it says what we want to say.

It's plain and simple: I love you and you love me. Lovers call it *Poetry.*
It's fundamental with or without melody. Lovers call it *Poetry.*

Sometimes it comes in a kiss in the moonlight at night shining down.
It's the language of love on everyone's lips, cuz love makes this world go 'round.
Same-o, same-o; teachers call it history. Lovers call it *Poetry.*
Romeo said it underneath the balcony. Told Juliet, "It's poetry." [Easy, baby!]

It's plain and simple [yeah, yeah]. Ain't nothing hard about it.
Cannot live without it [yeah]. Don't you know it's *Poetry.*

We live in a world where love's still a reason for living and
everyday when boy meets girl, another chapter of love is written.
It's easy, baby. All you got to do is be cool. It's easy, baby.

It's plain and simple: I love you and you love me. Lovers call it *Poetry.*
It's fundamental with or without melody. Lovers call it *Poetry.*

You know, living isn't easy but love is. The work is hard, the rest is short.
But it's finding someone to share it with ya. That's what makes it worthwhile.
[You know what I'm talking about.]

Plain and simple. Fundamental. Elementary. Sweet and gentle.
Warm and tender. Sentimental.

KRLA
Edition
BEAT
Volume 1, Number 36
LOS ANGELES, CALIFORNIA
15 Cents
November 20, 1965
It's As Easy As 1-2-3 For Len Barry – p. 6
Pick the Best Records of 1965 - p. 15

# Elision

# just my own opinion

I'm still out here singin' my ass off, if you please
High and kool and clean like a soft, warm summer breeze
But it ain't about the notes no mo' or a catchy melody
An' it ain't about no clever quote or some lousy poetry

I wrote a song about what's wrong
'Bout how most folks are livin'
Don't 'spect y'all to sing along

it's just my own opinion

Life's not about no iPhones
or selfies, don't you see
Ain't about no hype or Skype
or high technology
It's about carin' for someone else's needs
It's about standin' up for what ur soul believes

It's just my own opinion, but it sure feel like it's right
It's just my own opinion, but it keeps me up at night

Fifty-one percent's a majority
Ten men make a minyan
It's just my own priorities

it's just my own opinion

I'm still out here singing, my sound ain't grown old
I'm still bringin' it with a thousand pounds of soul
But I don't sing no songs ain't got no meaning
Ain't da time for nursery rhymes, dese kids is out here bleeding

I'm reachin' out, teachin' now
Livin' on a mission
A college fulla knowledge
An' ain't no damn tuition
Democracy 'posed t' be for all its people
But da dollar hollers constantly "all y'all ain't equal"

It's just my own opinion, but it sure feels right on time
It's just my own opinion from a highly troubled mind
Two-thirds is plurality
Ten men make a minyan
We done lost our morality

# I CAN'T SING

I can't sing — so I rap
I can't dance — not one tap
Got no chops — I can't act
But it don' matter 'cause I'm black
I can't sing — so I rap
Later for that 9-5 trap
Hard work — ain' where it's at
Manual labor — that's for saps
It ain' nothin' — but affirmative action
A guilty conscience — world reaction
For what they did — once upon a time
To those great-great-gran'folks of mine
Put 'em in chains — sold 'em as slaves
But actually — in reality
Ain' got nothing to do with me
But if I wear it on my sleeve
An' keep on keepin' on make believe
Someday — I just may
Have a star on
Hollywood Boulevard
I can't sing — so I rap
I can't dance — not one tap
Got no chops — I can't act
But it don' matter 'cause I'm black
And you did us wrong — you dirty rats
Ya can't deny it — facts is facts
For all those years — we sang the blues
Guess I could go to school
But education — that's for fools
So I'll open my trap 'n'
Keep on rappin'
"Dumb bitch" and "F- you"
Hurt whoever I wants to
And one day — I'll fool y'all
At Radio City Music Hall
An' one day I'll sell my soul
At L.A.'s Hollywood Bowl
At Wembly Stadium and
da London Palladium
I can't sing — so I rap
I can't dance — not one tap
Got no chops — I can't act
But it don' matter 'cause I'm black
Hey, if I may — some more truth
R&B means rhythm and blues
Y'all need to — face the fact
R&B ain't rhythm and black
Y'all don't own it — got no deed
It's everybody's property
And someone please explain to me
What the hell's with BET
Miss Black America — that's just sick
It ain' down — it ain' hip
Black girl and white girls
It's one planet — one world
Hey, I was raised by Smokey and James
The Miracles and The Famous Flames
I grew up on The Midnite Show
In Harlem at The Apollo
I ain' black — but y'all can bet
I'm damn sure close as you can get
*So to all my angry black friends*
*Now's not the time for revenge.*
It's over — It's done — You won
**We all did**

a dream that's lost its mind
a church without a steeple
liberty gone blind
her people still unequal
past partly fiction
future's cloudy, hazy
it's not democracy, it's

# DEMOCRA-CRAZY

self-congratulation
for a feat not yet done
constant celebration
for a war not yet won
claiming a peak of
a mountain never climbed
another fancy speech
a poem that don't rhyme
once a definite
now a shaky maybe
it's not democracy, it's

a child that's lost its way
come from 'cross the sea
a nation done gone insane
wishing world war three
unworthy candidate —
***dying to be king***
promises of great —
***lyin' 'bout everything***
another election —
***one more inauguration***
tradition repetition —
***a privilege bein' wasted***
our founding fathers fathered
a beautiful strong baby
named Democracy,
now

# IT'LL NEVER BE THE SAME AGAIN

I grew up in the record industry. Singin' songs I wrote myself for me.

I lived my life deep in R&B. Honorary Brother. Sista Lover. Dat was me.

Singin' soulful songs. Funky, young 'n' strong. Bad in bed.

Smokey was my idol. Billboard was the bible dat I read.

Board of Education and racial integration. Alabama drama way down South.

Blacks stood proud 'n' tall, Jack and Bobby changed it all

and the South very slowly came around.

JFK and Jackie made the perfect, lovin' couple

'til trouble burst the bubble down in Dallas.

Right turned to wrong, Camelot was gone

as the country cried and tried to meet the challenge.

But Lyndon Johnson made
Vietnam a grave and
fifty thousand kids wound up dead

The country that we loved
Is crumblin' t' dust and
**It'll Never Be The Same Again**

Now we got a guy who
worships dollar signs and
don' show nobody no respect

But he ain't all dat's wrong
It's been coming all along
and the curse is the worst is coming yet

'Cause once you damn a dream
'n' dilute what you believe
it's senseless t' just endlessly pretend

'Cause life might keep on livin'
But da dream will still be different and
**It'll Never Be The Same Again**

# I'mma singer

I'mma singer, not a thinker.
But a thought done cross my mind:
How can democracy and capitalism survive
side by side?

I'mma singer, not a thinker.
So I cannot comprehend: Whatever did
become of all dem damn red men?

I'mma singer, not a thinker.
But sometimes I do wonder:
Does thunder come from lightning or
lightning come from thunder?

I'mma singer, not a thinker.
So I really do not know: When we
destroy this planet, where the hell we gon' go?

***I can hit every note and sing any song.***
***But I do not know what makes love go wrong.***

I'mma singer, not a thinker.
But let me ask you this:
If the gift of life ends in death,
is it really such a gift?

I'mma singer, not a thinker.
But if I had a choice, I'd sing with my heart.
My soul would be my voice.

I'mma singer, not a thinker.
A voice, not a brain.
But I question the suggestion
that love is just a game.

Y'all think ~~~ ***I'll sing***
You work ~~~ ***I'll chirp***
You be genius ~~~ ***I'll be bird***

I'mma singer, not a thinker.
Don't know the meaning of life.
But while your stomach churns and you toss and turn...

**I'mma asleep like a baby tonight.**

Everyone is sleeping
It's the middle of the night
But the moon is my sunshine
It's the Light That Lights My Life

The stars don't simply twinkle light years away
They're like a million children gigglin' while they play
The black sky hides the hatred that jealous people feel
And the lies they tell each other with words that ain't for real

Lightin' crackles 'cross the darkness 'n' warns a storm's about to start
Thunder rumbles moments later like a bass drum in your heart
But the danger's not my nightmare, even evil people sleep
The nightmare strikes in broad daylight, blue skies kill the peace

With the dawn they'll wake up yawnin' as the calm comes to an end
Minds that once were dreaming will start schemin' once again
Heads of state will contemplate what their next move is
Their generals will warn them 'bout threats that don't exist

Stealth will fill the skies with planes that disappear
Built to kill with ordinance whose real weapon is fear
Russians will be rushin' to get their borcht and bread
In Tel Aviv they'll be relieved not to wake up dead

Mecca will beckon to Muslims everywhere
to come to the Kabbah and Ramadan in prayer
ISIS will frighten whomever they can
Tribal suicidals wagin' war without a plan

The British will consider the unimagined thing
Somehow, some way may come a day a Brother will be their king.
Taiwanese and Red Chinese lookin' for a fight
Crazy Neo-Nazi's hatin' everythin' ain't white.

Dawn 'til dush dey cuss 'n' fuss, same ol' sick-ass game
P.M. means Pure Madness. Daytime is INSANE.

Give me dark, give me stars, take the afternoon
Y'all can fight in bright sunlight, I just need my moon

Keep your cotton clouds And sky blue skies
Take your picture-perfect Lyin'-ass disguise

P.M. is pure yours
A.M.
Means
ALL
MINE

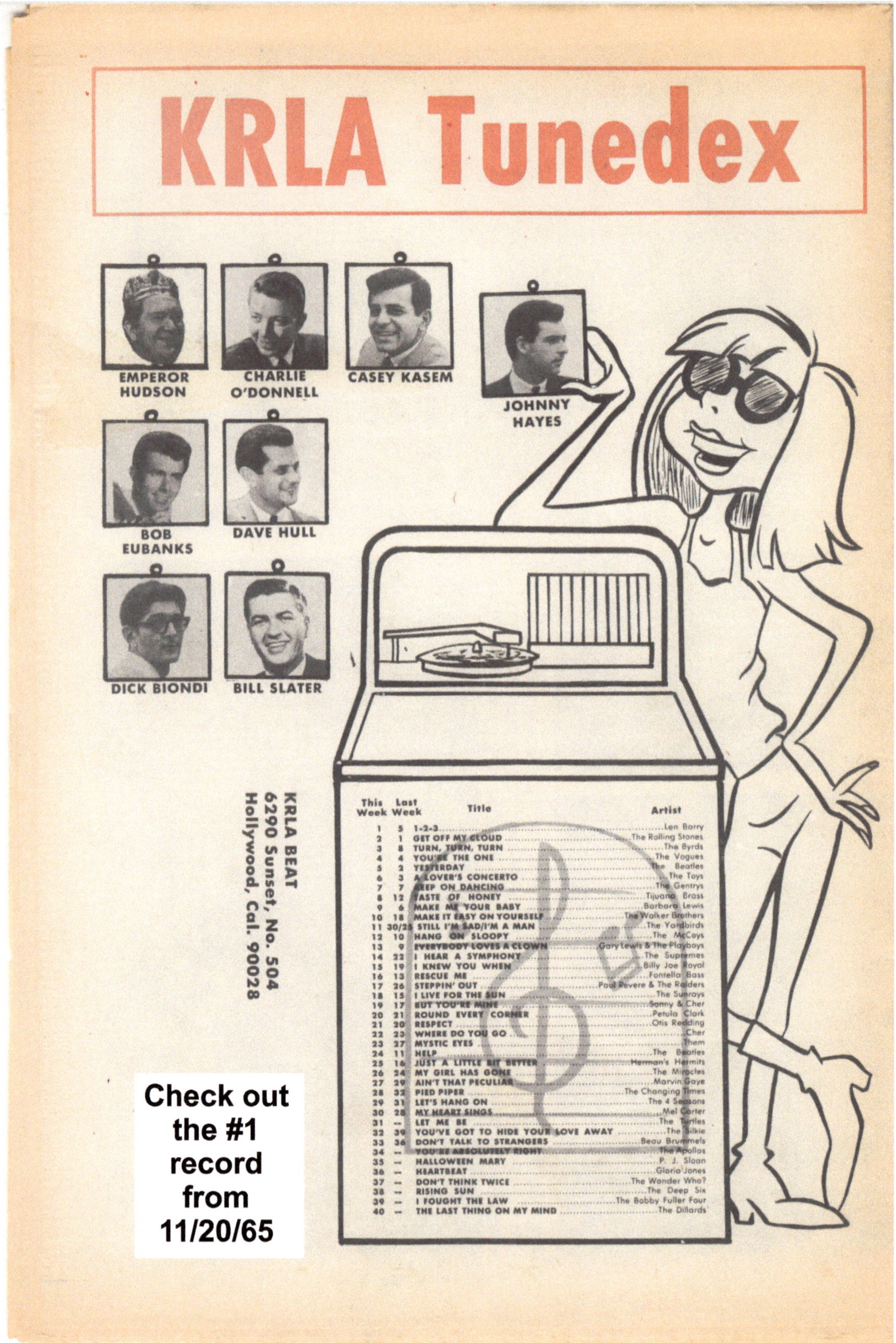

EMPEROR HUDSON

CHARLIE O'DONNELL

CASEY KASEM

JOHNNY HAYES

BOB EUBANKS

DAVE HULL

DICK BIONDI

BILL SLATER

KRLA BEAT
6290 Sunset, No. 504
Hollywood, Cal. 90028

| This Week | Last Week | Title | Artist |
|---|---|---|---|
| 1 | 5 | 1-2-3 | Len Barry |
| 2 | 1 | GET OFF MY CLOUD | The Rolling Stones |
| 3 | 8 | TURN, TURN, TURN | The Byrds |
| 4 | 4 | YOU'RE THE ONE | The Vogues |
| 5 | 2 | YESTERDAY | The Beatles |
| 6 | 3 | A LOVER'S CONCERTO | The Toys |
| 7 | 7 | KEEP ON DANCING | The Gentrys |
| 8 | 12 | TASTE OF HONEY | Tijuana Brass |
| 9 | 6 | MAKE ME YOUR BABY | Barbara Lewis |
| 10 | 18 | MAKE IT EASY ON YOURSELF | The Walker Brothers |
| 11 | 30/25 | STILL I'M SAD/I'M A MAN | The Yardbirds |
| 12 | 10 | HANG ON SLOOPY | The McCoys |
| 13 | 9 | EVERYBODY LOVES A CLOWN | Gary Lewis & The Playboys |
| 14 | 22 | I HEAR A SYMPHONY | The Supremes |
| 15 | 19 | I KNEW YOU WHEN | Billy Joe Royal |
| 16 | 13 | RESCUE ME | Fontella Bass |
| 17 | 26 | STEPPIN' OUT | Paul Revere & The Raiders |
| 18 | 15 | I LIVE FOR THE SUN | The Sunrays |
| 19 | 17 | BUT YOU'RE MINE | Sonny & Cher |
| 20 | 21 | ROUND EVERY CORNER | Petula Clark |
| 21 | 20 | RESPECT | Otis Redding |
| 22 | 23 | WHERE DO YOU GO | Cher |
| 23 | 27 | MYSTIC EYES | Them |
| 24 | 11 | HELP | The Beatles |
| 25 | 16 | JUST A LITTLE BIT BETTER | Herman's Hermits |
| 26 | 24 | MY GIRL HAS GONE | The Miracles |
| 27 | 29 | AIN'T THAT PECULIAR | Marvin Gaye |
| 28 | 32 | PIED PIPER | The Changing Times |
| 29 | 31 | LET'S HANG ON | The 4 Seasons |
| 30 | 28 | MY HEART SINGS | Mel Carter |
| 31 | -- | LET ME BE | The Turtles |
| 32 | 39 | YOU'VE GOT TO HIDE YOUR LOVE AWAY | The Silkie |
| 33 | 36 | DON'T TALK TO STRANGERS | Beau Brummels |
| 34 | -- | YOU'RE ABSOLUTELY RIGHT | The Apollas |
| 35 | -- | HALLOWEEN MARY | P. J. Sloan |
| 36 | -- | HEARTBEAT | Gloria Jones |
| 37 | -- | DON'T THINK TWICE | The Wonder Who? |
| 38 | -- | RISING SUN | The Deep Six |
| 39 | -- | I FOUGHT THE LAW | The Bobby Fuller Four |
| 40 | -- | THE LAST THING ON MY MIND | The Dillards |

Check out the #1 record from 11/20/65

# Verse

# DAMN BED'S TOO BIG

Quaint ain't a word
That describes a
lot of space
But quaint can be
even better
Like when we shared
quaint together

I loved rubbin' up
against you
When my lips gently
kissed your neck
Or when you
turned around
Crawled up 'n' down
Then rested your head
on my chest

I never needed
more room
Or time to be
by myself
I always viewed
solitude
As a sneak peek
into hell

Love does not
need Texas
Or a desert to
stretch out in
Even a closet was
big enough
For you 'n' me to
get down in

But now this
damn bed's too big
And there's just
too many pillows
Ain't nothin' but beer
in the fridge
L-i-t-e cans
by Miller

Yes, now this
damn bed's too big
'Cause it's oh-so-cold
and empty
Don't need no queen size
or king
Even a cot would be
plenty

Yes, now this
damn bed's too big
For loneliness to fill
'Cause a broken heart
That's torn apart
Don't need to sleep
on silk

Yes, now this
damn bed's too big
Guess I best face the fact
Dat dis ol' home's
Just a house now
'Cause love ain't
coming back

# RAINBOW

Once
I saw a rainbow
That was
lightning in disguise

Like
Honest Abe's shady pages
of little white lies

Like
in my bed when you smiled
and said
Until the day you died

Well, rainbows don't strike trees
Good souls don't deceive
And lovers shouldn't lie
To one another

But I guess
I understand
He's a much more
Stable man
Handsome, rich,
and thin
So go on
Claim your prize
Gaze up into
his eyes
And tell
your
lies
to
him

All that's left of me 'n' you
Is your fabulous face on my tattoo
With eyes that burn and lips that yearn for kisses

All that's left of you 'n' me
Is a heart carved in an ol' oak tree
Where the two of us pledged this love I'm missing

How did we blow it, how did we throw it away
Have you reached for tomorrow while I'm still stuck in
Old Yesterday

It hurts to give up this once-upon-a-love
on my chest
It's torture to kill the hope that there's still
something left
But now my tattoo is bruised black 'n' blue
And in pain
And our carved initials are so superficially lame

Yeah, all that's left is this ol' tattoo
On my chest
I'm so afraid that one day it'll fade
Like the rest

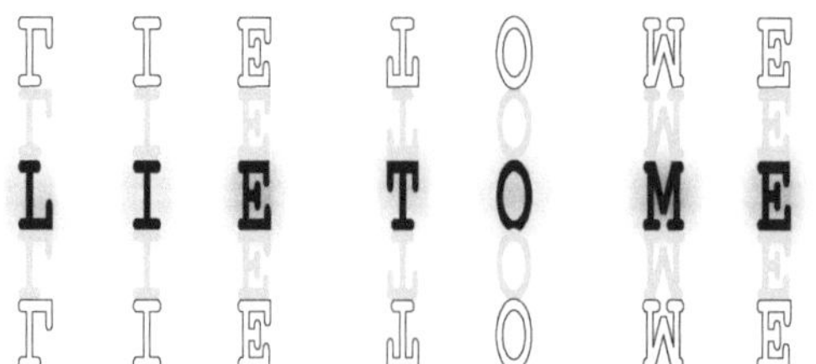


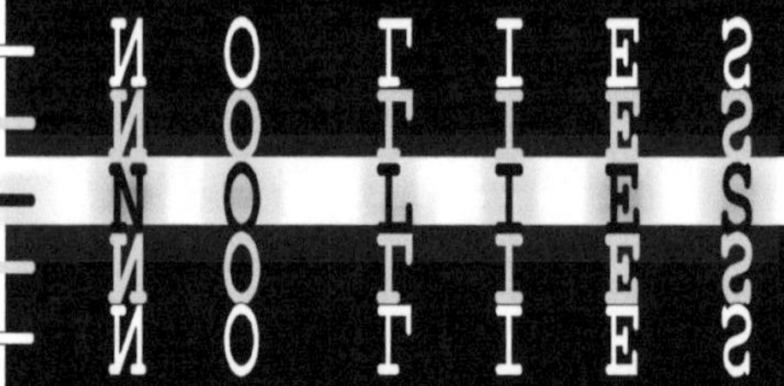


It may not be hip
It may not be wise
But ev'ryone fibs
Tellin' little white lies
It's not your whole life
It's just da edge
What good is the landin'
Without standing on
The ledge

The truth is so predictable
But lovers need surprise
Don' want to be convincible
Lie to me — no lies
Look into my eyes
Lie to me — no lies

Don't swear to God
Don't cross ur heart
Fibbin's part of livin'
Lyin' is an art
Don't wanna sleep
I wanna dream
Please excite my life
Hustle — con me — scheme
The truth is ideology
Fake-ass state of mind
Don' want me no apology
Lie to me — no lies

It may be B.S.
The little white kind
One whopper that unstoppable
From blowin' up your mind
Don't worry 'bout deception
Pain done made me wise
I don't need protection
Lie to me — no lies
Love done made me blind
Lie to me — no lies

It may not be hip
It may not be wise
But ev'ryone fibs
Tellin' little white lies
It's not your whole life
It's just da edge
What good is the landin'
Without standing on
The ledge

The truth is so predictable
But lovers need surprise
Don' want to be convincible
Lie to me — no lies
Look into my eyes
Lie to me — no lies

Don't swear to God
Don't cross ur heart
Fibbin's part of livin'
Lyin' is an art
Don't wanna sleep
I wanna dream
Please excite my life
Hustle — con me — scheme
The truth is ideology
Fake-ass state of mind
Don' want me no apology
Lie to me — no lies

It may be B.S.
The little white kind
One whopper that unstoppable
From blowin' up your mind
Don't worry 'bout deception
Pain done made me wise
I don't need protection
Lie to me — no lies
Love done made me blind
Lie to me — no lies

# monday morning

It was nine-ish and dreary. Be-better-if-it-would-just-rain dreary Monday morning. Another lousy, cloudy, Monday morning just like the many other late-May Monday mornings he'd been through. Once, at least some of them were different. Gotta get outta here. Ugh, it hurts. Hangover different. Ain't had many of them for a while. Damn. Wasn't really nobody left to have 'em with. Truth is, he'd never had many friends. No old cronies from boyhood or wild teens he once hung out with. Nah, those relationships always cost some small, clumsy favor, in the end. Ladies, special love ladies, layin' next to him all snug and satisfied after a weekend of sex, sweet passion, and promises. Well, those ladies were from another time. Long-gone, blessed yesterdays when mutual sacrifices still made sense. Nah. This was an I'm-alone-all-alone-lonely-and-lousy-on-a-damp-and-cloudy Monday morning. Oh, wow. He'd almost forgotten this Monday morning in May was Memorial Day. Damn. All dem dead kids who threw it all away. All dem Black kids dying for a freedom and equality that didn't exist. A spoken, lofty goal that long ago had deteriorated into some recruiting slogan displayed on a desk just above a drawer with an almost empty bottle of Jack sliding around belonging to some craggy, red-faced Master Sergeant. Ah. Oh well. The world was what the world was. Wasn't nothin' he could do about it. At least, thanks to his dad, he had money. He couldn't really picture goin' through all these miserable Mondays broke, too. This was hard enough as it was, he thought, catching a quick glimpse of the beginnings of a sprinkle on his big bedroom's beautiful reinforced picture window on yet another miserable Monday morning. "Donald?" came the voice from just outside his double-duty door. "You ready yet? You got that ten o'clock with the Israeli ambassador." Beginning to scurry, he thought, ah yes, guess I best dressed.

# EV'RYTHING

Ev'rything a poet writes don' rhyme
Comedians ain't funny all the time
Ev'ry chick that's pretty isn't fine
All dudes don't look good in Calvin Klein
Ev'ry corprit lawyer ain't dirt
Some have even done pro bono work
Ev'rything that glitters ain't gold
An' ev'rybody born black ain' got soul
All presidents ain't presidential
And 1-2-3 ain't always fundamental
Sometimes winter feels a lot like spring
See, ev'rything ain't always every thing

Ev'ry "I love u" ain't always true
And blues songs aren't always blue
How they feel is really up to you
And the mood your soul is going through

Ev'ry chick that's hip isn't Nicki
Y' gotta chill and be a little picky
An' da sistas don' always do it better
Sometimes white chicks got it together
Ev'ry Vladimir is not a Commie
Sometimes Commies have names like Tommy
Fights don't always happen in a ring
See, ev'rything ain't always every thing

Ev'rything ain't always every thing
It's all about the attitude you bring
Ev'rything ain't always as it seems
You ain't got to go to sleep to have big dreams

Ev'rything ain't always every thing
You
don'
always
get to leave
with
what
you
bring

# WAITING FOR WEDNESDAY

Wednesday. Noon. The early October autumn sun, while no longer hot, was still

too damn bright.

The old white guy rolled over, first to one side, then the other, finally waking up. Actually, both those inferences are a bit incorrect. The old white dude wasn't exactly white 'cause ain't no body white, and especially not when age-related creasing sets in. Secondly, only his body was old. His mind and spirit were almost as young and aggressively vibrant as, well, as when he was young and aggressively vibrant. He stretched his still well-toned but no longer muscled arms above his head, but suppressed the naturally accompanying moan.

He didn't let it out because he didn't want to wake her. It was a well-intentioned but futile gesture. She too was up.

The young black woman rolled over and under his arm, wrapping her own right arm around his now almost totally grey chest. But she, unlike he, did moan.

"Oooo," she exhaled. "That was damn good, Baby."

Actually, two of those specifics ain't right either. First of all, according to her, she wasn't so damn young. He rationalized: *At my age, who cares?*

Secondly, she was not black. She was jet black with narrow green eyes above high cheekbones. Shark-white teeth framed her puffy, pouty, luscious red lips that begged to be kissed, but always after teasing a bit. And short, squeaky-clean, black cornrows, blondishly streaked, that were unchanged since she left Somalia at the age of eight.

She crawled up his chest, kissed him twice, and offered softly, "I'll make us some coffee, Babe."

He didn't stop her. Damn it! He wanted to, but he didn't. He wished she'd stay wrapped around him forever. But he let her go, always enjoying the sight of her long, tight, beautiful black body bouncing out of bed almost as much as when crawling into it.

Shortly, the aroma of coffee filled the apartment. It was easy to fill. It was small. It had to be. This was New York, the city, and his best earning years were behind him. This sort of one-bedroom sort of efficiency apartment was it for him. He basically survived on Social Security and syndication replay royalties. He'd done some TV series work, some soaps, and even a few films, one of which he wrote. He wrote a lot. Poems.

Novels. Short stories. Sometimes, he'd read them to her on those very special Wednesday afternoons.

Never dressing, she brought him a huge mug of black coffee along with her own. They shared a toasted bagel. She sat cross-legged and terribly, totally unconscientiously nude. As they shared breakfast, *The Bold and the Beautiful,* and a rerun of *Grey's Anatomy,* she gave him warm, wonderful kisses on his neck and face, which he returned.

That escalated, of course, into full-fledged, blown-up, steamy but very warm and gentle sex. He cradled her as carefully as eggshells he'd never bruise, let alone break. She straddled him, not like some wild woman, but like a loving lover, loving the ride for both of them. They exploded together and she collapsed flat onto him. Chest to chest, and slept again for almost two hours. Her black, sweaty body slept with effortlessness, while he reached for recovery, having had enough for another wonderful Wednesday afternoon. She woke, kissed and lightly squeezed him.

She whispered, "I gotta go, Babe."

Jumping up, she pranced to the bathroom, quickly brushed her teeth, and slowly showered while she sang Bruno Mars' "Versace". She didn't sound like Bruno, but then again, Bruno didn't look like her.

She dried herself and came out towel-less to sit on the edge of the bed, cornering it, and began to dress. She then made up in the little mirror she'd brought from the bathroom, overdoing it totally — too much makeup, eye shadow, and terrible pink lipstick. He'd once sounded her about that, to which she coyishly replied —

"The white guys on the street ain't into basic black, Babe."

Still, even now, he thought looking at her, she's beautiful.

Putting on her very high, high heels, she came to the side of the bed where his spent body lay, bent down and kissed him. She reached over and picked up the the handful of twenties he'd left her on the night table, and, shaking her head, dropped it into her knockoff Gucci bag. The money fell softly, nestlin' between the lethal little .22 automatic and the pack of prophylactics she always carried.

She toddled away. At the last moment, she turned her pretty little face back over her shoulder and cooed, "I love you, Baby."

He half sang, half cried, back, "I love you, too," as the door softly closed on another week of waiting for

WEDNESDAY.

# DA GAME

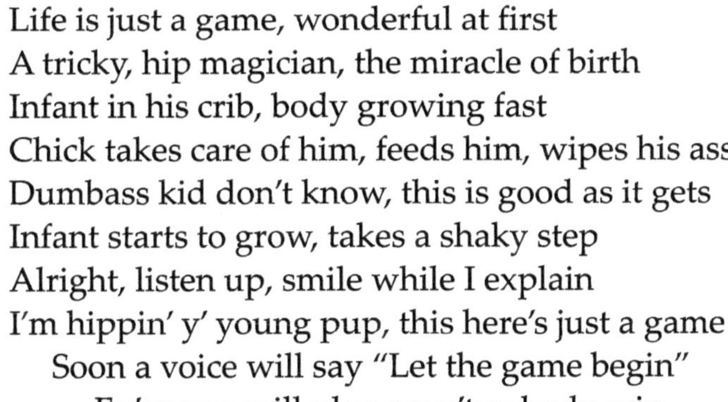

Life is just a game, wonderful at first
A tricky, hip magician, the miracle of birth
Infant in his crib, body growing fast
Chick takes care of him, feeds him, wipes his ass
Dumbass kid don't know, this is good as it gets
Infant starts to grow, takes a shaky step
Alright, listen up, smile while I explain
I'm hippin' y' young pup, this here's just a game
Soon a voice will say "Let the game begin"
Ev'ry one will play, won't nobody win
It's about da grumble, not about da roar
It's about de rumble, not da final score
It's about da contest, not who wins or loses
It's about da contact, ain't about da bruises
Ain't about how smart, it's about how wise
'Bout becomin' champion, not about da prize
It's about da shuffle, not about da deal
It's about da hustle, how it makes y' feel
It's about da smile, not about da laugh
It's about da naughty, not about da bad
It's about da boy, not about da man
It's about da fingers, ain't about da hand
It's about da ache, not about da pain
It's about da guilt, not about da blame
It's about the sinner, not about da shame
It's about the picture, not the fancy frame
It's about the sniffle, not about the sneeze
It's about believin', not what you believe
It's about the kisses, not about da lips
It's about da chitlins, not da fish 'n' chips
It's about da fiction, not about the truth
It's about da doubt, not about the proof
Ain't about da skill, it's all about the passion
Ain't how bad da kill, it's how good da assassin
Ain't about da lovin', it's about da love
Yo' give t' one another when de goin' gettin' tuff
Child, it's just a game, ev'rybody plays
Half a hundred years, a thousands nights 'n' days
It's just a crooked game, 'cause life's a phony friend
Don' matter how good ya play
We all lose in da end

# MY SKY

I see the sun and the moon as lovers
With the stars as their little kids
Where Halley's Comet keeps on comin'
As each new day begins
Where the Milky Way
Is where they play
'cause heaven's where they live
Hey, don't tell me
It ain't real
'n don't tell me
What I feel
'cause
It's my sky — my canvas
It's my sky — so listen, damn it
I'll paint any real I see
'cause my sky
Completely belongs to me
I see Venus without clouds
And a Mars that isn't red
Where water flows in crooked rows
And all life ain't quite dead
I see Mercury's fleet wings
Sweep the universe
Saturn without rings
And Pluto kissed the Earth
So don't tell me
What is and isn't
No don't tell me
It's my vision
Hey
It's my sky — 'n I beg your pardon
It's my sky — 'n I'm the artist
And one thing rings so true
That my sky
Does not belong to you

I see a planet without war
In a world of love and peace
Where science finds a brand-new cure
For each brand-new disease
So don't tell me
What's possible
Achievable
Accomplishable
'cause
It's my sky — my scene
It's my sky — my dream
And one thing's plain to see
That my sky
Just belongs to me

PHOTO CREDIT: NASA

# Ad Lib

# AM I BLACK ENOUGH?

I can sing like Michael, Bruno, and Drake. I can run like Smokey, Tupac, and Drake.
Now, you're my lady, so pretty in black. And I love you, baby, that's where it's at.

But am I black enough for ya?
That's the question I ask.
Am I black enough for ya?
Can you struggle like that?
Am I black enough for ya?
Tell me I know it feels.
Am I black enough for ya?
Am I keeping it real?

Tell me, how you're mama gonna react when you bring me home and I ain't black?
And, girl, what you gonna do when the brothers and sisters turn their backs on you?

But am I black enough for ya?
That's the question I ask.
Am I black enough for ya?
Am I up to the task?
Am I black enough for ya?
Do I got enough jive?
Am I black enough for ya?
Can you feel me inside?

My pants ain't down around my butt. I ain't Timberlake. I ain't no chump.
I ain't the epitome of hip, but I ain't no punk like Robin Thicke.
I come from Philly, deep in the hood. Where it was UHN! and Bad meant Good.
Now, I'm your lover and you're the love of my life.
Inside I'm a brother,
but my skin's still white.

But am I black enough for ya?
That's the question I ask.
Am I black enough for ya?
Am I up to the task?
Am I black enough for ya?
This is a real love.
Am I black enough for ya?
Is my love enough?

This ain't about the world that all screwed up.
It's just about us and color-blind love.
It ain't about Black. It ain't about White.
It's about us and
The rest of our lives
So, tell me

# C'MON, MAN!

Bitches, ho's and pimps
Dat's your whole vocabulary
Mindless mental wimps
Going nowhere in a hurry
Pants down below your ass
Got no sense — got no class

Think u a bad man down wit' da funk?
You don' understand you just a punk
Running your line on
young, dumb chicks
Time after time fatherless kids
Big bad dudes high on meth
Truth is y'all all scared to death

**Historically speaking,**
**I'm down with the rage**
**But the time done come**
**to just turn the page.**

M-F this and M-F that
M-F everything dat ain't black
Violence thrives on
nighttime streets
Hungry five-year-old
can't eat

Original gangstas
dead and gone
Mothers cry for
sons gone wrong

Hangin' on corners
selling grass
Get hip to yourself
dat time's passed
Affirmative Action's a
slap in the face
But take advantage
— EDUCATE!
'Cause enuff's enuff
time to grow up.

There's a new game in town
New rules in the hood
There's a new game in town
and it's time y'all understood
There's a new game in town
It's called common sense
There's a new game in town
Dumb stuff's got t' end

Today's kids be grown
tomorrow
What dey gonna be
Don't look back in
shame and sorrow
Take responsibility

**Historically speaking,**
**I'm down with the rage**
**But the time done come**
**to just turn the page.**

**C'MON, MAN — NO MO' GUNS**
**C'MON, MAN — NO MO' PUNKS**
**C'MON, MAN — NO MO' DRUGS**
**C'MON, MAN — Y'ALL BETTER THAN THAT**
**C'MON, MAN — LOVE YOUR LADIES**
**C'MON, MAN — RAISE YOUR BABIES**
**RUN. JUMP. DUNK. SING AND DANCE. BUT**
**C'MON, MAN, C'MON!**

# The Miss **Black America** Pageant

The Miss Black America Pageant
A contest whose concept is stagnant
The Miss Black America Pageant
Dat ol' kinda soul that's just tragic
There's a chick from California
Who's almost white
She could win it all
but she's **too damn light**
Miss Carolina's the **color of honey**
Mississippi's
all 'bout da money
Dere's a killa from Philly
Black as **night**
Whose green eyes gleam
Like laser lights
The Miss Black America Pageant
A contest whose concept is stagnant
The Miss Black America Pageant
A contest ain't
need to be happenin'
If there was a
Miss White America
Da bro' and sistas
BE
marching all
DAY!

C'mon man, get up off it
C'mon man, 's time to soften
What's done is done
It's in the past
Revenge tastes sweet
But it don't last
The Miss Black America Pageant
A contest whose concept is stagnant
The one down the shore
Ain't all white no more
**All shades wear the crown**
**Black 'n' White 'n' Brown**
C'mon man, think again
C'mon man, when do it end
Over is over,
Done is done
War been fought
Y'all done won
Miss Black America's on TV
Not BET, but NBC
C'mon man, **dis great nation**
**Said no-no-no to segregation**
So Miss Black America ain't
KOOL!
Separate ain't equal,
FOOL!

# Miley Makes Me Smile

Demi Lovato drives me crazy 'n' I love Alicia Keys
Hailee Steinfeld, that's my baby, and Halsey weakens my knees
I'm down with Camila Cabello and into Fifth Harmony
Bebe Rexha makes me mellow and Rihanna heats my dreams
but...
MILEY MAKES ME SMILE
Miley makes me laugh
Billy Ray's little girl
Trying to be so bad
Miley makes me smile
Miley makes me grin
Daddy's little angel
Actin' like Sista Sin

Ciara lights my fire and Ariana's grand
Selena Gomez is my bad liar and Beyoncé is top brand
Kerry Washington's my scandal and Lucy Liu's my word
Nicki Minaj is hard to handle and Gaga is absurd
but...
MILEY MAKES ME SMILE
Tickles my fickle soul
Acts like she's so wild
But she's in complete control
Miley makes me smile
She's so Country Cute
Innocence of a child
Yet forbidden fruit

# She Goes Both Ways

Sometimes she's aggressive
Sometimes she's passive
Sometimes it seems she's even proactive
My baby's a lady,
'cept when she ain't
Lovin', hating', part Satan, part saint
She can be cotton and she can be stone
She can be rotten down t' the bone
She can be candy
or icing on a cake
Whatever my needs are, whatever it takes
On top or da bottom,
she goes both ways
She's 50/50
No one gets the edge
She walks on a wire
She lives on a ledge
She loves pretty ladies
and powerful men
She is what she is, she doesn't pretend
She's a chameleon
feeling her way through the dark
with fire in her wires
and ice in her heart

# Sshhh Sshhh

Somewhere in Virginia
There's a ♥ carved in a tree
With his and her initials
For a love that could not be
He was free and white
She was not, just light
She was just a slave
He was royalty
But regardless of your power
You can't set pigment free
There were laws back then
'Bout how you had to act
And it stipulated clearly
White cannot love Black
But his heart couldn't read
And neither could his soul
And the feelings that he felt
He just could not control
He had vast ambitions
He wanted to achieve
But the mind cannot put limits
On what the body needs
She'd looked at him with awe
Since she'd been a kid
Damn the dumbass laws
She wanted to be his
He was in his forties
She was just fifteen
Most beautiful perfection
He had ever seen
Her skin was firm but smooth
A golden shade of beige
Her hair was silky soft
And fell down to her waist
Her eyes were neon green
Narrow, almost slanted
Sometime seeming mean
Forgiving but demanding
She had a bit of bitch
Which helped her to be brave
She spoke three languages
Lover — Mother — Slave
He told this baby nation
That slav'ry was a sin
But back on his plantation
One hundred slaved for him

He promised her her freedom
If she could just be his
He gave her broken promises
She gave him six kids
He loved her 'til his death
With his very last breath
He tried to keep it
— a secret —
Still ev'rybody knew
It was obviously true
They'd broken that taboo
Somewhere in Virginia
There's a ♥ carved in a tree
With his and her initials
For a love that could not be
That's Jefferson loves Hemings — true
And Hemings loves Jefferson — too
sshhh

TJ + SH

# True Love... at Last

She reached out her arm, stretched and spread her fingers. There he was. Oh, God, thank you! He was the love of her life. The touch of him. The sound of his strong breathing. The touch of his love made everything alright.

His love made the struggle, the fight for life, make sense. And oh! How she loved him. Had since first she laid eyes upon him. No man felt like him. No man smelled like him. She didn't have to guess. She knew.
Oh, she'd touched others — too many others.

If she was rich she'd lay with him all day, all night, like this. But that wasn't the case. They were not well off, so she had to go. She kissed him softly, lightly, so as not to wake him.

Then she put him in his crib
Covered him, tucked him in
She'd see little Timmy later on
But was getting late, she best be gone
Time for her to hit the bricks
Strut her stuff, turn some tricks

# Bridge

The X-15*s* zip-glided through the moonless, black night sky, disappearing and then reappearing from in and out of still, grey puffs of clouds. The US-made semi-stealth, swept-winged dart flew moderately on the wickedly hot September night at close to six hundred knots — one-third its capable speed. The pilot was a ruggedly ugly but somehow still attractive Colonel B.J. Bartlett. A crackerjack veteran of many mini-wars who looked quite impressive in his in-charge jumpsuit. He's sexy, she thought, as long as he flies with his helmet on.

*She* was the five-ten, seventh degree martial arts, sharpshooting, cold-blooded killer.

*She* was the stern-faced, knockout chick in the co-pilot seat.

*She* was dark, delicious, and boldly beautiful.

*She* was hard-jawed and cleft-chinned.

*She* was a chocolate, brown-eyed bitch.

*She* was Max Gold — soldier, assassin, and spy elite.

Max was originally short for Maxine, but now her peers agreed it definitely best represented *maximum*. Only twenty but lethally trained and finely tuned since she was thirteen, Max sat silent, helmet in lap, confidently relaxed.

A super soldier on a mission to kill.

Her once-long, black-brown wavy hair no longer framed her fierce face. It was topped, instead, with a Marine-like crew cut, high and tight.

As the nearly invisible X-15*s* quietly crossed the Iranian border, Max re-helmeted, stood and, after twice tapping B.J.'s fiber faceplate, signifying two minutes, she abruptly moved toward the rear bomb bay doors. Perched at the exit, the one hundred and twenty seconds seemed like an eternity. Crouching, waiting on the drop, she thought of her father, Joshua "Juno" Gold, the director who sent her on this mission to murder. This mission she didn't want, but he was the boss.

The bomb bay doors opened and Maximum Mossad dove out into the black sky above Tehran — Muslim hell.

Mossad is Mossad. There is nothing else, anywhere, like it. The CIA and KGB are kindergarten killers and grade-school intelligence and counter-intel agencies compared to Israel's Mossad.

Israel survives in the midst of an Arab world that collectively and adamantly denies its right to exist. From its infancy in 1948 under the Balfour Declaration, Israel has struggled to simply continue to breathe. Only the greatness of Theodore Herzl and David Ben-Guiron backboned its early refusal to acquiesce to hostile Arab pressure and U.N.-based world political mockery. Israel's diplomatic skills were essential in the fight for international recognition.

But, while the politicians jousted outwardly, behind the scenes Israel's survival, in the Middle Eastern bloodbath, was solely attributed to Mossad and the early, ruthless tutelage of its leader, Moshe Dayan.

Mossad agents are a combination of Chinese Shaolin's lethal martial arts skills and US Navy Seals' discipline; their agents a fantasy mix of James Bond and Bruce Lee. The best of these is Max Gold, but that knowledge wasn't helping her one bit as she landed on the ground. Hastily digging a shallow grave in the Iranian dirt, she buried her black parachute, jumpsuit, and backpack after first removing a Muslim woman's black jilbab.

Max would don that symbol of female subservience at dawn, magically transforming into Madame Muslim. But for now, ingesting a banana, stale dates, and orange juice in the rain-soaked, muddy mini-forest just outside of Tehran, she dug her heels into the slime, leaned back against a slim tree trunk, and copped some ZZZZs in a shallow sleep.

In the city, locked in the basement of an old mosque, Sam slept fitfully. His short, honed, muscular body needed relief. Sam was a gambler, a liar, a thief, and a traitor who compromised his family's honor and his country's faith — selling its secrets to cover bad gambling debts to bad people.

Sam was Mossad and fully aware he was a rogue agent whose future had no future. Sam the Gambler gambled that he and his money could somehow get out of Tehran before the floundering Iranian scientists found out the nuclear fission formulas he'd handed them were actually seven years old and outdated, irrelevant, and totally bogus.

However, it was not the Muslims Sam feared the most. Ironically, it was the Jews, his Jews. He knew Mossad inside and out. Damn, he was raised by Mossad, mentored night and day by the director himself who would relentlessly hunt him. No one knew the director, Juno Gold, like he did. After all, he was his son. Sam Gold!

Make no mistake: Sam was a well-trained and highly skilled package. He was no Shaolin Master or Bruce Lee, but he would be no easy prey for just any Mossad agent. So, his nightmare-within-a-nightmare was that the frozen heart of Juno, his father, would send his best, the best-of-the-best, his half-sister.

Max.

After Sam's mother died, Joshua had a prolonged and in-depth relationship with a transplanted African Jew, Kendra, Max's mother. The Nubian beauty eventually went home to Nairobi to escape the growing dominance of an evolving Joshua into Juno.

Max only knew her mother through pictures and, from her cohorts, innuendo-laced flattery of her beauty. Juno and Kendra never married, so Sam could never legally call her stepmother. But Kendra had been in his home and life, day and night. More importantly, she was in his heart.

His mother was dead.

His country was in peril.

His father was as cold as the glaciers of Juno, the ice capital of Alaska from which he got his moniker.

Sam was the joy of Kendra's life...until she gave birth to Max. Max took up more of Kendra's time, attention, and heart than Sam wanted to yield. Still, when she fled Israel, Sam was decimated.

Max, at thirteen, was like her father, stoic. A teenage, lethal-lightning, young, proud patriot hell-bent for Mossad. Activated at seventeen. By nineteen, setting the new standard for all Mossad agents to live up to.

Max woke from her mini-sleep, soaked by rain, steeped in mud, and fully aware of her miserable mission. Her father had sent her to kill his son, her brother who, unbeknownst to anyone, she had loved deeply all her life.

Max inhaled a flask of cold coffee, cleansed herself, and quickly donned her Muslim garb. She took a deep breath, reluctantly ready to attack her mission — the juxtaposed horror of Love versus Duty. The last thing she did was pull out a gold neck chain from her peasant smock. Two things dearest in her life hung from it. She kissed the Silver Star of David, and then opened the the gold locket to kiss a faded picture of her mother.

Tehran!

In person it was as it was on film Max had watched ad-nauseam. Simplistically busy, but she'd seen outdoor markets and backfiring buses since she was a kid when Kendra took her to Tel Aviv. Max warily negotiated her way through the hustle and bustle of Iran's capital until there it was. The mosque was old and worn, right where Israeli intel said it would be. Guarded by radicals dressed as holy men, kinda like armed imams. How would she get in?

She purchased a bucket and mop from an old woman in a private, wordless sale and, head down, headed for the mosque's entrance. The guards nodded to a veiled and limping woman, shared a snide inside joke between themselves, and waved her in. She wanted so badly to take off their heads, but she stayed in character. She limped her way to the basement and approached the locked door where two men, outwardly armed, stood guard.

One look and she knew the "bucket bit" wouldn't work on those two. They were serious. Not joking. Not welcoming. Still, they had no chance. She gave them none.

Max crushed the knees of the tall, heavily-bearded man with lightning heel kicks. So fast it could have been almost simultaneously, she took out the other man's left leg with crushing heel thrusts. Immediately they were incapacitated. With a quick twist she broke second man's neck, then stabbed the first one in the heart with his own knife. They died on the floor. She pulled her silenced .44 auto and fired three dead-on, quick bursts blowing the locks on the heavy, crusty door.

Inside the cell, Sam had heard the noise of sudden quiet and silent death, and he knew. The door flew open and there she stood, this nun-like Muslim woman, gun in hand. The veil did not hide his sister. He said nothing. She raised the .44 and aimed it at his heart.

In quiet anger, she blurted, "You friggin' idiot."

She dropped her aim and deftly shot his leg chains apart.

"Turn to the side and hold out your arms," she commanded.

He did so and she blasted his handcuffs off, freeing him, and sharply hid her weapon.

"Whew," Sam said.

"Did you think I was going to kill you?" Max said, lowering her veil.

Sam shrugged. "Yes."

"So did I," Max retorted. "Now put the short guard's uniform on. It's clean. That's why I broke his neck."

"Figures," Sam jested. "Only you."

"Cut the bullshit," Max interrupted. "We gotta get out of here or you'll wish I would've shot your dumb ass."

"Where we going, hero?"

"Home. I'm taking you home."

They hitched a ride on a beat-up, twin-prop clunker and bounced around in grey storm clouds for hours. Exhausted, three days later they stood before Juno Gold. The director of Mossad — master, mentor, and father — stood and glared at his children.

He raged at Max. "You disobeyed me!"

But he had known all along it was going to be a rescue mission; she would never kill her brother.

"He's here. You deal with him," Max retorted. She turned and exited without another word.

The EL AL DC-8 glided in and out of beautiful, puffy, white clouds, and slowly started its descent. Max peered out of the portal and did something she rarely did: smiled!

This time, she wasn't Mossad.

This time, she wasn't Maximum Max.

This time, she wasn't coming to kill.

This time, she was coming to love: Africa, Nairobi, and most of all, Kendra...

Mom.

1-2-3
DECCA
LEN
BARRY
INCLUDING:
1-2-3
LIP SYNC
TREAT HER RIGHT
WILL YOU STILL LOVE ME TOMORROW?
LIKE A BABY

# TWINITY

YEAR: 2085 A.D
PLACE: OUTER EDGE OF MILKY WAY GALAXY
TASK: JUMP TO GALILEO GALAXY
MISSION: FIND HABITABLE PLANET

Damn!

Stuff flew by the window like the wicked wind warning of a summer storm about to tear Tulsa apart; that is, if a childhood memory didn't exaggerate it. Tulsa hadn't been home long. In just a blink it was a used-to-be fleeting foothold for the first five years of a shaky start. Chicago was next, then Detroit, Boston, Pensacola, and finally Washington, DC, where Dad was discharged.

The Army had pushed Dad around like an old, rusty robot without the will or the license to resist. He, in turn, had dragged his family from temporary to temporary until the limits of his pension permanently placed them at 120th and Amsterdam Avenue in New York's Spanish Harlem.

Dad was most honorably discharged as Master Sergeant Dirk Little Page, who'd amassed thirty years in the Hemisphere Service. He'd been wounded three times and wore multiple medals that he made sure were quite visible in all the photos taken in full dress. Unfortunately, that was all that remained of Dad and his stalwart military legacy. Dad died on his sixtieth birthday, having rewarded himself for that achievement with the present of a free-fall skydiving gift of death when he fell free from sky to ground, torn chute streaming behind.

It was ironic that for someone who'd spent so much of his life packing, he surely didn't pack his chute very well that day.

Dad's dad, Granddad, was a full-blooded Cheyenne, Native American, Wyoming State Policeman, whose father, Great Granddad, was the last reservation tribal chief. Dad's wife, Mom, Keyasha, was Sudanese, African. Therefore, their only child, our Little Page, was Black African-American Indian.

So yes, this Little Page, our Little Page, paused briefly, glimpsing out the window as the sky flew by. Well, it really wasn't just a window. It was a giant porthole and our Little Page was Lt. Commander J.J. Little Page, fondly called "Butch" by her crew.

This Indian splib kid's ship was the W.H.S.S. Extraprize. Make no mistake, this was Little Page's ship and Little Page was captain. The one-and-only-order-giving, staunch, rigid voice that mattered. And be sure this Harvard cum laude, Annapolis-trained thirty-two-year-old Navy product was tough. Butch was a bitch.

Yes, she was a bitch. Lt. Commander J.J. Little Page was a five-ten, hard-bodied, bold, brown, Western Hemisphere Navy superstar. She'd flown stealth jets off jet-powered flat tops for years, acquiring multiple commendations for her astounding carrier career.

She'd been to war, eventually commanding a stealth wing of six that torpedoed and depth-charged guerilla subs in two furious, undeclared conflicts. She'd posed quite a sight in her full dress whites on the deck of the W.H.S.S. Kennedy when receiving the Navy Cross for action beyond-the-call from Majesty Rasheed Robinson, the third such titled Western Hemisphere Chief, long after the last presidency.

Her neon glass-green eyes gleamed with pride on that memorable midday, summer, sun-drenched event.

Back then she flew in the blue. One thousand miles per hour. Up to one-hundred thousand feet. But the sky flying by now was black and no longer sky, but space. The W.H.S.S. Extraprize had covered outer space to the far very edge of the Milky Way Galaxy, leaving behind even the distant planets, Uranus and the re-confirmed Pluto.

The Lt. Commander thought they would soon initiate the jump on her command, from their home galaxy, through the vacuum of space to the Galileo Galaxy. Thrusting toward the planet Twinity, so named because it appeared to be Earth's double through the magic of the Super Telescope Hubble 3.

Except for the brief stardust show she'd just observed, the intergalactic journey had gone well, so perfectly well. After turning the watch over to her first mate, Little Page returned to her quarters to be just plain Butch for awhile. Once there, and after pouring herself a small snifter of Courvoisier Brandy, she enveloped herself in her huge, soft leather recliner and silently autobiographed her journey of ascension. She introspected and realized that the miracle of miscegenation had created an explorer who was part Columbus and a greater part Shaka Zulu, the indomitable African warrior.

It was 2085. The youngest-ever astronaut thought this was not merely to be a curiosity-based exploration. No, the Western Hemisphere had honored her to captain the W.H.S.S. Extraprize to scout for a possible new home for Earthlings in the future. Unfortunately, that future, it appeared, was not to be a very distant one.

The warnings of global warming at the millennial turn of the century were now manifesting into full bloom. Polar ice caps were melting, resulting in rising tides worldwide. Great ports and harbors needed rethinking and ongoing rebuilding. The Grand Ol' Lady, the Statue of Liberty, was now knee deep in polluted saltwater eating away at her. Globally, wheat fields were burning up as well as cornfields and even potato crops.

Science had searched the universe and finally found, hopefully, a match. So there she sat, soon to be blasting past the Galileo Galaxy's sun.

"Captain. Captain," the pretty ensign semi-whispered. "It's time. It's time."

She woke from a shallow doze and calmly responded, "Yes, dear." She gently stroked the soft, smooth skin of the rookie's face. Springing upright, she directed, "Tell Lieutenant Liss to throttle back to half-full. And muster the ship's company."

"Yes, Captain," replied the baby-faced ensign, smiling, imagining how unique this was about to be.

"Go, Crissie," the captain chided, poking the ensign's turning behind.

Butch made way to the command deck and enlightened her crew. She used only her natural, unamplified voice to inspire and assure them. "We are about to go where Columbus, John Glenn, and Alan Shepard have gone before — into the unknown. Don't be afraid. Be excited. Don't be hesitant. Be aggressive...but be careful.

"Listen to me. When I direct you, you do it. When I compliment you, smile. When I don't, do it better. You are the best Hemisphere has and I am the best of the best. No matter how critical a moment may be, I refuse to lose even one of you."

She paused to let her words sink in, then continued, "I want to get where we're going, but only if we all get there. I am your captain, your lover, your father, and your mother. You are my children. We are the Nina, the Pinta, the Santa Maria, the Spirit of St. Louis, and Noah's Ark. Our brothers and sisters have loused up our planet. So they have sent *us* to find a new one. A new home."

The crew stood straighter, prouder while their captain went on.

"We will not disappoint. There are kids back there, innocent infants who've done nothing wrong; destroyed nothing. They have a right to life. We will warp, we will jump, we will land, and we will explore. Be careful. Anticipate, but do not expect. Where there is water and oxygen, there will be life. That is what we know."

She looked each crew member in the eye and drilled her next point home. "What we don't know is everything else. We must love and respect one another. How you feel about each other, and most of all yourselves, is how you will be perceived. Listen. To. *Me*. Do. Your. *Jobs*. Do. *Not*. Ad lib. *Trust* me. I *love* you."

The entire crew, the whole gang, smiled and applauded. "Dismissed!" she barked. Another killer "Butch Talk" had delivered its magic.

Lt. Commander Little Page sat in her leather bridge chair, downed a huge cup of energy, coca-coffee, and for the next thirty minutes focus-studied her charts, committing them to picture memory.

"On my mark," Butch directed. "All ship's company set time watches to top of the hour. Ready? Mark."

She turned to Lt. Tonka, "Set course to ninety degrees by twenty-six minutes."

"Aye, Captain. Ninety degrees by twenty-six minutes," Tonka confirmed.

"Steady for seven seconds, Tonka. There it is. That's the worm hole. Go to warp drive three and prepare to jump on my command."

"Aye, Captain. On the lean," came Tonka's affirmation.

"Engineering, pull light, be prepared to curve it and stunt gravity on my jump command. Ship's company, secure yourselves for sixty seconds – and gravity void on my jump command. Tonka! Three. Two. One. Jump. Damn it, now!"

The Extraprize shook violently, suddenly, and then abruptly calmed to an eerie suspension. Everything that had not been secured, floated. Stardust, thick and swift, shot by the foot-thick front steel glass with a speed never before experienced by many aboard. For an endless moment there was no sound, no movement, no laws, no rules, and strangely, no fear. Then it all went black. No stars. No dust. No nothing.

The front glass showed...nothing.

It was like a giant blindfold suddenly covered up the universe.

After a mini-lifetime went by, a thin snow-white mist replaced the black. Then, from the snowy mist came the blue and the brown and the green. Yes! There it was. A beautiful ball of life.

Twinity!

"Tonka! Listen up," Little Page directed sharply. "Reverse warp drive. Power down to thrusters. Steer zero-zero degrees and achieve orbit."

She turned her attention to Science. "Science! Drop all probes, barometers, thermometers, atmospherics. I want to know everything. Wind. Temperature. Oxygen, nitrogen, hydrogen. And a specific gravity reading. If there are oceans, I wanna know tides. Salt or freshwater. Repeat. I want to know it all to the finest measurables."

She was roaring now and on she growled, "Communications! Send out signals. One-hundred-eighty degrees. Not three-sixty. Play music. Bach, Brahms, Vivaldi. No hard core and do not try to communicate."

She then issued commands to the entire complement. "Everyone. I repeat: Anticipate. Don't expect. Relax, but don't chill. All y'all be aware. She looks beautiful, but so do female lawyers."

The amazingly similar data arrived. All the survival vitals came back, if not exactly comparable, certainly livable. Except for the thick dense cloud cover that made visual verification possible.

Still, now it was time to send notice back home. "O.H Communications! Lt. Collins, get me Earth. Western Hemisphere. Panama Base."

Lt. Commander Little Page
sat back in her leather
to get it
all together

She had done it
gambled and won it
She had flown
where none had gone
Reached higher
and warped on

The Afro-Injun chick
had flown this hero ship
past the last horizon
glidin' flyin' drivin'
Now Daddy's little girl
had found a brand new world

What would it be like?
Was it worth the flight?
Why hesitate, why doubt?
It's time to go find out
So once more she barked
"Tonka, take us down."

Shuttle Xtrek struggled free from the Extraprize. First roaring, then gliding, before firing retrorockets and backing down. Searching for brown ground, its speed lessened on approach to the beautiful blue-green planet. First Mate Collins was left to command the Mother ship. The shuttle crew was small:

- Little Page, Lt. Commander (official representative of Earth)
- Tonka, Lt. (second in command)
- Christine, Ensign, Ultimate Translator. (Would they need?)
- Mr. Roberts (doctor)
- and Jones (with stungun laser-pulse, if needed)

The shuttle circled and hovered. Little Page inhaled the scene out the window and marveled at the beauty of Twinity. So green. So blue. Huge fields of long green, dotted by wheat and grain, beached the shores of freshwater lakes. There were also saltwater oceans as the probes had reported, along with relating that the gravity was kool as were the nitrogen, hydrogen, and oxygen levels. There would be no need for space gear. They would need no E.V.A. suits, no helmets, no oxygen tanks.

## "THE XTREK"

The exit side door opened. She stepped down and out, followed by the small crew. She strode slowly toward a greeting party, advancing with staunch magnificent rhythm as the wonderful smell of green grass filled her Cheyenne, brown proud, Injun brave, straight nose.

Butch, with magnificent rigidness, slowed then stopped, facing a greeting team of smallish, blonde fresh-faced males and females, uniformed but hatless. Young, vibrant militarists. They were fronted and led by an even shorter but much older woman, graceful, warm-faced, and silver-grey-headed. When all had come to rest, the porcelain-skinned grey lady folded her arms and spoke in a thick dialect heavily-accented in a British-like military staccato.

"What brings you here?" she voiced. "What is it that you seek?"

The Lt. Commander offered, "We are from the planet Earth. Third from the sun in the Milky Way Galaxy. I am—"

The old woman interrupted Little Page. "We are fully aware of your planet and its problems."

Little Page, graced softly and continued, "We have observed your planet, as well as the fact that it is almost Earth's twin. We are here in peace and awe. We seek only friendship."

The brown beauty nodded in abeyance, looked around her and continued. "We love your lakes and your grass. We are amazed by your beauty. We wish only to co-exist."

The pale-grey leader, half turning away, glanced back over her shoulder and barked only three words.

"Go home, nigger."

The pole was gold, shiny and slippery, extending from the ceiling to the mirrored stage floor. The reflection that jumped from the base up to the top was not a mere image but a vision of impossible perfection. Her tall, tight body sensuously stretched most of the pole's length, alternating between climbing it like a cat, and slithering down it in slow, torturous twists and turns like a snake without its rattle.

Her beige body was long, rare considering she was Oriental, Asian as far as anyone knew. Actually, she was American, Chinese-American, born right there in Baltimore only a few blocks from the infamous Charles Street strip where she was now — stripping.

The faces on the bodies that sat at the bar didn't care if she was Chinese, Japanese, Burmese, or alienese. The minds behind the eyes that leered and lusted weren't thinking about where she was from, just where she was taking them.

She was the twenty-two-year-old daughter of Wang and Wahzi. Immigrants who worked night and day. All their lives in their laundry. But the fools on the stools didn't care.

She was in her second year of medical school. A brilliant student on her way to becoming a pediatric surgeon. But the burning brains at the bar didn't care about that either. No, all that counted was the trip they were taking together; she the driver, they the passengers.

She had decided. Upon graduation she'd go back to China and give herself to the kids of the Old Country. But that didn't matter here, not now, to these men. All she was to them was the jet black hair, luscious lips, and fabulous face of a stripper.

She was a person. A student. A daughter whose real name was Zhang Zi'. But to the frenzied fanatics who gaped as she teased and tantalized as she took off her top, Zhang Zi' didn't exist. No, they — lost in fantasy — stood, cheered, hollered, called out to her by the only name they knew

— mako —

The music at Club Chaos grew louder and heavier as the cigarette smoke grew thicker. Drumbeats blasted faster. The faster they went the slower Mako moved. Like molasses on a stick, she enticed the men who mentally mauled her. She oozed across the misty floor as their eyes followed like hungry bloodhounds. She showed them plenty of skin to keep them in sin. She would take off no more.

The dancers hated the club. The smell. The smoke. The men they seduced. All they saw were men, middle-aged and married, marauding as pimps and princes in their own delusional, dirty dreams.

But Zhang didn't feel that way about them. She didn't condemn the men for being into her body because she was into it too. When she danced, she wasn't just seducing the guys. She was seducing herself. One day, she thought, I will be Dr. Zhang Zi', too busy saving children to dance for men. But right now, for the time being, there was something she loved about being

— mako —

The room was white. Bleached white. Sterile white. Super-bright radium lamps bounced off caps, gowns, and masks, filling the operating theatre with white cleaner than the whitest cloud on the brightest day. Two p.m. said the clock on the balcony wall just below the viewing glass. Eight hours since the operation had begun. It had been almost a decade since her days as a dancer at Chaos Club. But this room wasn't some flaming stage on the strip in Baltimore.

No! This was a critical stage in an operating room in the People's Hospital of Shanghai.

Just as she'd promised, Zhang had returned to China, her homeland, and dedicated her brilliant skills to giving life back to children who had all but given up hope of living. She'd become famous, revered, almost worshiped by the Chinese. Especially by the doctors and nurses she worked with — even though her Chinese language skills were minimal.

She'd saved hundreds through the years, but that didn't matter now. Not to the nine-year-old girl on the table. Everyone called her Little Ling-Ling. No. All the other lives she'd saved were history; only this one mattered for now.

Removal of a tumor in Ling-Ling's brain had gone more slowly than expected. Dr. Zhang Zi' first tried a minimally invasive procedure: she drilled a hole in the skull hoping to burst the growth and drain it. But it was too big. The skull would need to be opened and Dr. Zi' would need to go in.

The child remained awake during the initial attempt. But now she was put to sleep under a general anesthesia. This was not good news.

"Suction! More suction!" Zi' barked in English to her bilingual staff. And work they did. Blotting. Suctioning. Transfusing as the skillful surgeon carefully cut the terrible tumor away.

Suddenly, hemorrhaging increased!

The child's heartbeat decreased!

Her pressure fell!

Eyes darted above masks and a silent panic began. They were losing Little Ling-Ling. But Dr. Zi' was unflappable.

"Double suction. Thirty cc's adrenaline. Raise her feet," she directed. "Someone wipe my face. And calm down."

And they did. Guided by her uncanny ability and concrete confidence, they watched the magnificent magician push on for hours through the treacherous touch-and-go.

Finally, she looked at the clock. It was six fifteen p.m. She said, "Dr. Chow, you may close."

"Yes, Doctor," he responded in English, eyes dropping, and bowing in respect.

Eleven doctors and nurses hailed the amazing American with gloved applause. Dr. Zi' took one look around the blood-spattered room, then walked out. She pulled off her bloody gloves and gown.

She was the epitome of excellence and class. On the table was yet another child whose life she had saved. Yes, Little Ling-Ling would grow to be big. She smiled as she dropped her gown in a container...

The pole was gold, shiny and slippery, stretching from a mirrored ceiling to a sawdust floor that only partially hid the beautiful body that kicked at it and crawled through it. She was who they had all come to see this evening at the Poo-Poo Club, Shanghai's supreme strip club.

They were mostly married, these Chinese men who stared at her and fantasized. The other girls, dancers, hated them. But she felt, as she always had, like she was seducing herself. Now she did so by slowly, sensuously rising from the dusty stage while boldly unbuttoning her top. Her beautiful naked breasts fell free, just as she was free.

A nasty little smile licked her lips as men shouted her name because now she knew the truth about herself. Yes, by day she would be the esteemed Dr. Zhang Zi', Pediatric Surgeon. But in the naughty of night her soul would wrap around a gold pole. And there, in the smoky darkness, she would always be

— mako —

©cpc-8657-26
COLUMBIA PICTURES presents
CHUBBY CHECKER in DON'T KNOCK THE TWIST starring GENE CHANDLER, VIC DANA, LINDA SCOTT,
THE CARROLL BROS., THE DOVELLS with LANG JEFFRIES, MARI BLANCHARD, GEORGINE DARCY
A FOUR LEAF PRODUCTION

LADY
brave

"Squaw!" he bellowed. "My soup is cold."

She bristled. My soup is cold. My eggs are hard. My meat is tough. My potatoes are lumpy. My this. My that. Everything's always my.

"Me warm it, Colonel," she offered as she leaned down to pick it up, slightly brushing his long blond hair that he doted on daily. Carefully she lifted his bowl, again barely touching his shoulder as she did. She smiled to herself, knowing full well that both accidental contacts were only two more of many she intentionally initiated daily. It titillated both of them.

She felt him tighten up, being both defensive and stimulated at the same time. "Stop it, squaw," he said. But she imagined him whispering You're making my dick hard.

Her people called him Yellow Hair. He was tall, strong, and arrogant, but handsome for a White Eye. She fully enjoyed torturing him. He was George Armstrong Custer. Soldier, colonel, and killer of Indians — her people, the great Sioux Nation. The Sioux once covered the West as did the buffalo whose meat nourished them and whose hides warmed them and formed the walls of the teepees sheltering them from summer's dust and winter's harsh, cold winds. Her mighty tribe was now confined to the Black Hills of Dakota as the buffalo had gone to wherever shrinking multitudes flee to escape the searing bullets of hundreds of White Eyes who killed for profit — or worse, for sport.

She was not like the other officers' servants, squaws who looked at her with disdain and admiration. She was beautiful. High, sharp cheekbones accentuated narrow, piercing black eyes that flashed equally with the fury of love and hatred. Her fierce face was framed by hair, long, silky-smooth, flowing, pitch black, and touched only by the red scarf headband she wore pulled tightly above stern eyebrows accentuating the silent rage in her eyes.

She hastily reheated his broth and returned to the dining room where she carefully placed it in front of him. Insidiously, she touched his semi-clenched right hand as she did. Sitting at the head of the table was one highly self-esteemed General Crook. He quietly noticed her touch and smiled to himself, but for different reasons.

That would be the last time the pompous Yellow Hair would feel her touch. That night, late, when clouds crept across a dimly flickering early-summer moon, she would escape the fort's tortuously damning subservience to return home to her tribe where she would report. Yes, her fake servitude allowed her to be privy to specific observances important to her people.

She rode wildly on a stolen cavalry stallion. She carefully covered his hooves to render her escape soundless and untraceable. The black horse ran bravely but was nowhere near as swift as Paint, the magnificent pinto that awaited her return. She rode hard and swift with the unbridled aggression she'd shown since childhood. She had excelled in every phase of warrior skills usually reserved only for braves. She could outride, outshoot, and outfight her male counterparts. She was the lovely, lethal, warrior woman, ultimately renamed Lady Brave.

She was born Blue Sky, the youngest granddaughter of Sitting Bull. She learned to crawl, stand, and run like a deer alongside the tribe's other wild child. He was Crazy Horse and would grow to be the only warrior as deadly as Lady Brave. They rode together, hunted together, raided together as one. She at his side as the only warrior woman in the Sioux Nation. She didn't cook or make babies. She killed and made war!

Now she rode rapidly, bursting into her tribal village to the wild adulation of the quickly doubling and tripling Lakota and other tribal allies. By Sitting Bull's large tent lit with many fires, she spotted Crazy Horse and excitedly jumped into his heavily muscled arms. They entered the tent of the Sioux Nation's leader and sat by the fire across from him.

Sitting Bull rose on aging, shaky legs to welcome them and quickly sat back down. He opened his hands, nodded to his granddaughter, and finally spoke. "Tell me of the White Eyes, my beloved. Tell me of their numbers, their weapons, the skill of their soldiers, and the wisdom of their leaders. But mostly, my youngest, tell me of their will."

Slowly rising, she said, "They are many, but not as many as we are becoming. They are highly trained, my Grandfather Chief, but not finely skilled. Their leaders are strong but neither they nor the soldiers are willed as we. But one, Custer, he of the yellow hair, has the will of our bravest brave and the heart of a Sioux warrior."

"Tell me of him, he that you are taken to," a wise Lakota chief beseeched.

Lady Brave continued, "My grandfather, he is tall and strong, brave but foolish. He is a leader of men who admire his bravery and fear his risks. They follow in wonder of where he is going and why he makes such haste. Other officers hate Yellow Hair, but not Crook, the general of generals. He sees the value of Custer's bravery, but will not ride with him."

She looked around the circle. "Yellow Hair dares danger. Many times charges ahead even of his scouts. He is easy to see. He does not wear the uniform of the White Eye soldiers. He wears white buckskin and big hat from which arrogant eyes of hatred seek the path of our people."

Sitting Bull said, "You know him well, Blue Sky. How is it you have crawled into his mind so?"

"I was his squaw servant, Great Chief. I serve meals. Shine boots. Sew holes in scrawny wife's clothes. He talk freely around me thinking I speak only few words of his language. He treat me like squaw slave, but I play with him like child with a toy in dirt outside teepee."

"Is he to be feared, my child?"

"No, Warrior Chief. He is to be baited, tempted. Trapped! He rushes into a tomorrow that will not be his."

Sitting Bull rose slowly and clearly announced his intentions to the circle. "We will wait for our brothers, the Arapaho and the Blackfoot, to grow our numbers. Then we will dangle honor and afterlife for Yellow Hair to charge in to. White Eye soldiers will follow. I will watch from the hills above Bighorn as all die."

He turned to Lady Brave. "You have done well, my granddaughter. Now, go and wait. Eat, drink, and share the tent of Crazy Horse's love 'til it is time. Your brother braves shall set trap and then, together, from the ground above, we will watch Yellow Hair and his soldiers meet their ends."

The tent of Crazy Horse, warmed by the fire, was warmer still from the fire of his hatred stoked by jealousy. "I will do battle with Yellow Hair and kill him myself," he raged, swaggering by the fire.

"Be careful, my husband," Lady Brave chided. "He too is a warrior."

Crazed, Crazy Horse asked, "And who would you want to survive?"

"My love," she replied, "I hate him as I hated the Arapaho and the Blackfoot before they have suddenly now become our brothers. Our numbers grow with those I do not trust."

"We are plenty. One Sioux brave is worth ten White Eyes," he said, thus ending the conversation.

*******

The next days and nights were filled with the pounding of drums, puffing of chests, and the making of wild love that, for a time, chased the doubts and soothed the soul of Crazy Horse. At times, Lady Brave became Blue Sky, but never let sexual subservience cloud the reality that she was a lethal killer, every bit the death dealer her husband was. She was not a romanticist. She didn't gaze at the stars or caress flowers of the springtime bloom. She spent her days riding Paint and making new poison-tipped arrows for the bow. A bow she made herself to be strong and flexible.

She was against fusing with the Arapaho and Blackfoot and ignored them in the village. Her prowess was well known by them and they were happy to be ignored.

On the morning of the fifth day, the drums stopped and the tribe awoke to the reality that the time for ego building was over. It was now the time to kill or die. All knew a victory at Bighorn would not stop the coming of White Eyes from the East. All knew that eventually their way of life would surrender to a tomorrow of annihilation — or worse: dismal, captured survival on a reservation, fenced in and kept to memories of yesterday's freedom that would never return.

But this was not that. Not yet! This was a chance for one last victory. A chance to at last drive White Eyes from the Black Hills that miners, prospectors, and their protective soldiers had so recklessly invaded. Thousands of painted braves kissed their families goodbye and rode slowly to the hills above Bighorn. Sitting Bull, still steady on horseback, led the first group. Crazy Horse and Lady Brave led the second, which included a select group of Blackfoot raiders who would bait the doomed bluecoat cavalry to its end. Yellow Hair would charge into the myth of conquest and eventually be left to die in the midst of the reality that victory belonged to the Sioux.

Lady Brave sat on Paint. She had red lightning bolts streaking across both cheeks toward her nose painted black down its length. She rode bareback and barelegged except for two loincloths, chest barely covered with deerskin tied loosely behind her neck and back. Tucked at her waistband were a tomahawk and long knife. An arrow pouch was slung behind her right shoulder next to her heralded bow. Her army repeating rifle sat back in the teepee.

Lady Brave would bring death with the weapons of the Old Way.

The small but deceptive Blackfoot raiding party descended slowly, crossing the Little Bighorn plains and approaching the shaded soldier camp. It stopped at the banks of the river and did not cross. Oblivious to the raiding party, there sat Custer in a rare meeting with his officers as his two hundred eighty five troop cavalry drank late-morning coffee. But the bluecoat scouts were aware and quickly informed the fringe-frocked colonel of the perilous Red presence

"Troops! Prepare to mount!" Custer commanded.

The 7th Cavalry scurried to finish dressing and stood prepared to jump on their horses. "Mount!" came the order and the troops did just that.

But not the scouts.

"Go no more," the head scout informed. "Not cross sacred burial ground." But that was a lie. He was Blackfoot and recognized the markings on the raiders' horses and braves. Instinctively, he knew the whole force would be painted, raging braves of many tribes, all united under Sitting Bull.

Custer glared at them, stiffened in the saddle, and roared, "Forward, ho!"

The full 7th advanced at a trot, crossed the river, and pursued the raiders who cleverly managed to barely keep their distance…the bait had been cast, the hook was in, and the end was inevitable. From the campside of the river, scouts watched soldiers disappear into a dust cloud and knew they would never see them again.

The trot turned to a gallop as the 7th, swords drawn, raged after the raiding party only to see them be absorbed by Sitting Bull's massed army suddenly appearing atop the northern hills.

Custer's eyes bulged in surprise. He thought there must be thousands, never suspecting he'd only seen half of what faced him. The 7th pulled up, sheathed their swords, and raised repeater rifles. Down from the hills came Arapaho and Blackfoot with Sitting Bull's Lakota Sioux leading the whooping, hollering mass.

"Fire at will!" commanded Custer, outwardly calm but secretly hoping the new army repeaters would even the score. The men of the 7th, still mounted, fired again and again, mostly without aiming. There was no need. A thick wall of rage surrounding the soldiers was closing fast.

Many of Sitting Bull's warriors fell, but most did not. Their bullets and arrows tore into what now seemed like a small force of harried, wide-eyed White Eyes. The troops were being cut to ribbons.

George Armstrong Custer was no longer calm. He screamed commands.

"Dismount!"

"Regroup!"

"Form up!"

But Yellow Hair was still hopeful. That is, until he saw the western hilltop with the second mass of Indians exploding down onto the Little Bighorn flats. Sioux! Arapaho! Blackfoot! Thousands, mounted and on foot, roared and raced into a history that would quickly become legend. White Eyes fell by the tens, ripped apart. The second wave, mostly Lakota, attacked fearlessly, jumping over fallen brother braves and surging into a ravaged bluecoat mass that hardly fired back. As a last resort, the now undisciplined soldiers fired only with side arms.

High above, Sitting Bull watched from the north. Lady Brave and Crazy Horse watched from the west. Suddenly the warrior woman could no longer simply watch. Custer had been hit. She'd seen it. Still, he was alive and firing wildly with his right hand; his left side hung limply after twice being shot. She kicked Paint and blasted wildly down into the flats. Crazy Horse followed. They charged into the doomed bluecoats around Yellow Hair. She leaped from Paint and, now flat on his back, straddled him.

Knees planted firmly at his armpits, she quickly pulled her long knife and snatched a new poison-tipped arrow from its shoulder pouch. She glared at him and, in a controlled rage, said, "Soup no cold no more, Yellow Hair."

His soon-to-be-dead eyes recognized her in horrible amazement. Blue Sky bent down, slowly lifted his chin, and kissed his lips with all the passion they'd both long known. She sat up. Raised her right hand and plunged the poison arrow deep into George Armstrong Custer's heart. She grasped her long knife tightly and took the yellow hair from Yellow Hair.

She closed his dead eyes and stood, waving his scalp, proudly proclaiming, "The devil is dead. I am Lady Brave, blood of Sitting Bull, and I have killed him!"

Crazy Horse, still mounted, watched from a few feet away. He saw her passion and wished only that, one day, she could hate him like that.

There's a white chick in da hood
That the bros and sisters love
Forget the fact dat she ain't black
She's made o' da right stuff

Her mother died at childbirth
Her father got shot dead
Named da baby Shayna first
Known now as Sheena instead

She was raised by Kendra
Her dad's black lady love
Warm and kind and colorblind
Thick as brick and twice as tuff

They lived up in the ghetto
Where cop cars' sirens screamed
Loud and strong, all night long
Messin' wid young bloods' dreams

Sheena graduated high school
Number One
But deep inside she realized
Her climb had just begun

She took a flight to Hong Kong
Then jumped aboard a junk
Sailed her tail to ol' Shanghai
And found the Shaolin monks
They taught her heart martial arts
She hipped the monks t' funk

She studied, knuckles bloodied
Breakin' bricks and boards
Then hand t' hand, man t' man
She fought a thousand wars

By the time she left, she was the best
And thanked them for their help
They deemed her queen, she split the scene
A fifth-degree black belt

While there she studied herstory
At Shanghai University
She graduated school
Lady Cum Lauda, Suma cum kool

She came home hard and hot
Became a Philly cop
Who taught all the men
The art of self-defense

She started up some charities
After work on her own time
to grow some grass and plant some trees
And give the kids some pride

She built a boxing gym
With just a touch of class
With hardwood floors, rugged rims
And backboards made of glass

The bros call her bad
The sisters call her good
Universally known by the name on her throne
"Sheena, Queen o' Da Hood"

# *breed*

her great gran'ma was a Maasai mama
her gran'mom was a Chiricahu squaw
her mother was a great British princess
with a face dat rates a round of applause
*Shee's-a-breed*

her gran'pop was an Apache chief
he's the hatred dat be ragin' in her blood
her father was a Swedish scientific genius
who hipped her to experiment with love
*Shee's-a-breed*

The super-smart, giant heart that beats
in a Viking squaw dat's never known defeat
she's the Bittersweet kiss from the lips that I need
*Shee's-a-breed*

a breed is a mixture dat grows into a fixture
in your soul
a whole lotta hot mixed wid a smidge
o' freezin' cold
a little left, little right, a little black, a little white
a brat whose act just cannot be controlled
*Shee's-a-breed*
a chick whose trips from all aroun' da world
who's kiss is different from da other girls
from hundreds of branches and thousands of leaves
she's the queen of her genes
*Shee's-a-breed*

November 20, 1965 THE BEAT Page 6

WRITER TURNS SINGER

# Fortune Smiles On Len Barry

"It's as easy as one, two, three" . . . Len Barry is heading straight for Hitsville.

His face is familiar, 'cause you've seen him as lead singer for the Dovells; his sound is great, and his record is headed toward the top; his future is the brightest, 'cause he's got a lot of talent. With that as an introduction, then, let's take a look at dynamic Len Barry: past, present, and future.

*Past:* He was born June 12, 1943 in Philadelphia, Pa., where he was graduated from high school and went on to attend one year at Temple University on an athletic scholarship.

### Good Faker

His formal musical training has consisted of "the Musical College of Hard Knocks out here on the road," although Len claims that "I *fake* very well! I fake drums, guitar, sax, a little bit of bass, and some mouth organ." That's some kinda faking, Mr. Barry!

Len has been writing music for about three or four years now, and says, "I think that writing is much tougher than performing, because sometimes you don't get the self-gratification out of it—because you don't get the same acclaim as the artist that recorded your song, even if it is a hit. It's a lot tougher to be successful as a writer than an artist."

### Sound Background

In the *present,* Len has a great sound going for him, but it isn't something which was simply delivered to him for Christmas; he has been developing it for quite some time:

"As far as a distinctive, or an individual sound goes—I don't know if I have one yet, but I hope to acquire one. Now, I think it's more or less of an R 'n' B sound with Negro overtones that I've gotten from performing for four or five years on the road with mostly Negro tours."

Len has a great deal of interest in everything that is going on about him in the present, and he has some very definite ideas about such present people as one Mr. Bob Dylan:

### "Real Genius"

"I think that as a writer he is brilliant; I think he has a genius—I mean actual, flagrant genius that you can touch. As far as these protest records are concerned—predominantly the Barry McGuire record and the Dylan things—I think that in reality, they are speaking the truth and these problems *do* exist and they're not saying anything against the grain of what's actually happening. But I don't personally believe that it should be said 20 times a day on the radio."

Len is a man of firm conviction, and he eagerly told *The BEAT* of his own personal favorites in the field of entertainment:

### Favorites

"My personal favorites—I have very few, but I'm firm on them—include Sammy Davis Jr. I think he's great, and I enjoy him; he's an entertainer's entertainer. But I think if it hadn't been God's will, in a few years Sam Cooke would have been the greatest entertainer that ever lived. I also enjoy the Miracles, Mary Wells—the entire Motown label."

What does the *future* hold for Mr. Barry? Len is very thoughtful and concerned about this, and he shared some of his ideas with *BEAT* readers:

"Every man that *is* a man, has personal ambitions; and I'm glad to say that I'm no different. I'm very common where that's concerened. I love people and they don't frighten me. When I was a little boy, my mother once told me—'Don't be afraid of people because they're only here to help you; and if you give them a chance they will.'—and I've found this to be true.

### Future

I would like to be an established entertainer and while I'm having my hit records, the world is very, very rosy—but I know that someday it's gonna be a lot tougher to get them, probably, and I'd like to establish myself as an act. I'd just like to help people forget their troubles for a couple of hours, and establish myself in that way."

For that all-important *future,* there is an album—already released—appropriately entitled, "One, Two, Three," and possibly Len's next single will come from this LP.

Len Barry is a talented, outgoing, sensitive young man who is searching for his star, and his philosophy-of-the-road is one well-worth repeating:

### Return Favors

"I don't want to sound like a ham or anything, but everybody needs help in this world in order to make it, and I've gotten *more* than my share of help—not once, but *twice!* And it's very difficult to explain just how thankful and how grateful I am because I'm not really prepared to do anything else in life; and it's a very wonderful thing when you can make a living doing what you like to do. I would just like to thank the people—instead of protesting *against* them—Thank you very much for giving me a chance to live a good life!"

The pleasure is all ours, Len!

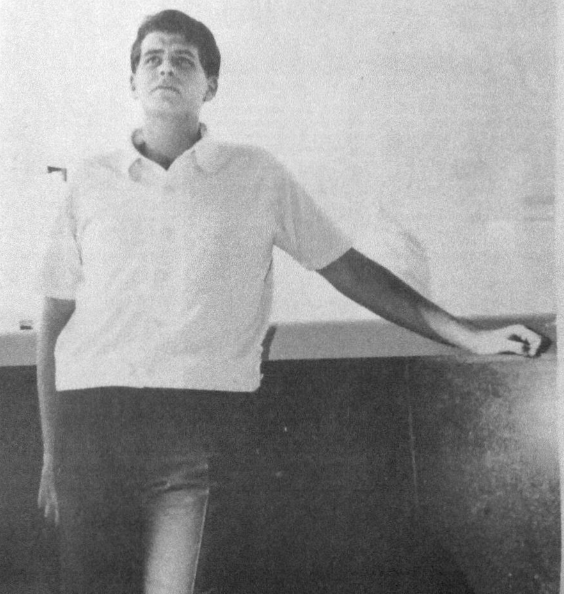

. . . LEN BARRY

# Gold Rush On Again

The gold rush is on again and the Beatles and Beach Boys are coming out ahead.

Both groups record for Capitol and both just received more gold records for sales over a million.

The Beach Boys just received their third and fourth straight gold disks for albums "Beach Boys Today" and "Summer Days and Summer Nights."

The Beatles added another one to their collection with the million sales of "Eight Days a Week."

# Liverpuddles

By Rob McGrae

Manager, The Cavern

American recording artist Ben E. King recently appeared at the "home" of the Beatles—The Cavern Club.

Interest in his appearance had been building up as his scheduled appearance drew near, but no one expected the scenes that we witnessed the night he played.

The Cavern is notorious as the place where the audience doesn't scream at any star, no matter how big he is. However, this night proved to be the exception.

A huge crowd was already forming at the club when Ben arrived. Some of the girls recognized him as he entered and it took six men to get him out of the midst of the girls and into the club.

### Ben Impressed

Ben was very impressed with the Cavern when he first saw it and was enthusiastically looking forward to performing on the stage. After introductions between Ben, Ray McFall (owner of the Cavern), Bob Wooler (the discoverer of the Beatles) and myself, we decided to show Ben around Liverpool.

We left by a side door to avoid his fans and took him to see the Liverpool sights. By the time we returned the club was filled with expectant fans.

### Taken Off Stage

The girls went mad when he got on stage and no one could hear what he was singing. The girls almost succeeded in breaking through the cordon of men protecting the stage and Ben had to be taken off the stage after only one number. The audience was warned that they would have to calm down or he would not come back.

After ten minutes he came back on stage and was able to complete four numbers before he had to be taken off again.

Ben was visibly overcome by the reception and asked if he could go on again after the audience was warned once more to calm down. He was finally able to do 35 minutes on stage including his hit songs "Amor," "Spanish Harlem" and "Ecstasy." He rounded off the chaotic show with a terrific version of "Twist and Shout."

Ben told me after the show that it had been the best reception he had received outside of America and that he would always remember his performance at the Cavern.

### Visited Another Club

We then went to another club in town called the ¡Blue Angel where a group called the Delmonts were performing. The Delmonts asked Ben and his guitarist, Jimmy Brown, if they would like to perform a number and they gladly agreed. The night turned into one of the best jam sessions ever seen in Liverpool.

Ben summed up his feelings at the end of the evening by saying that he would never forget his visit to Liverpool and intended to come back as soon as possible. I know that everyone here hopes that he does come back soon.

### Another Record

And yet another record was set by a Liverpool group recently when the Merseybeats appeared at the Cavern to try to set a world record for playing beat music. They performed a record 9½ straight hours of beat music before their drummer John Banks collapsed. They had hoped to play for 12 hours solid.

Even more impressive was the fact that they had just appeared on another show and had motored through thick fog to arrive at the Cavern at 5 a.m., when they immediately went on stage. The boys went for the first 3½ hours without even having to repeat a song and it was a first class show right up to the end.

Well, I'll be seeing you in this column next week so don't forget to be around.

# Chorus

JUXTAPOSITION

HEY, Y'ALL. LISTEN I'M ON A MISSION
JUST A POSITION JUXTAPOSITION

my snow white was jett black; 'n' I was the one layin' flat on my back
she kissed me and I sat up straight; she axed me baby do you feel ok
I mean your hair's a little nappy and ur skin's a bit gray (I said)
fine young thing, I'm kool now, one kiss, bitch, and damn man, wow
I pulled her back down and did her whole face, like she come from outer space
I licked her 'n' whispered wild child, listen, my whole life is a juxtaposition

**juxta-what? po-sition**
**juxta-what? po-sition**
**no rules. one condition.**
**no rules. one condition.**
**living life a-juxtoposition.**
**living life a-juxtoposition.**

HEY, Y'ALL. CHECK IT OUT. WOW.

everything I do is upside down, inside out and square is round
easy's hard, smooth is tough, I be breakin' alla rules to makin' luv
ev'ryday be night, night be day, workin' don't work, I be ready t' play
rock-n-roll and country ain' hardly for me, I'm stone cold soul and r&b
I do ev'rything I ain' suppose t', did it my way simply cause I chose t'
singin' my song, my own rendition, my whole life is a juxtaposition

**juxta-what? po-sition juxta-what? po-sition**
**no rules, one condition no rules, one condition**
**living life a-juxtoposition living life a-juxtoposition**

I sang at the apollo at just eighteen, was da culmination of a young blood's dream
da midnite show, a gray boy sensation, da bros and sistas gave a standin' ovation
I played wid james and the motown review, killed 'em in philly and out in watts, too
round 'bout den did nothin' by the books, found a new world and was definitely hooked
my white sails sailed 'n' I landed on black, no roun' trip ticket, wasn't turnin' back
irresistible force, unstoppable mission, my whole life is a juxtaposition

**juxta-what? po-sition**
**juxta-what? po-sition**
**no rules. one condition.**
**no rules. one condition.**
**living life a-juxtoposition.**
**living life a-juxtoposition.**

SAID WHAT I HAD TO SAY. LIVIN' MY LIFE, MY WAY
UPSIDE DOWN. SQUARE IS ROUND. BUT I DID IT.
CRAZY BABY. BUT I LIVED IT. LIVE YOUR LIFE AS YOU
SEE FIT. DON'T EVER RUN AWAY FROM IT.

# GOD

**God?** Oh, I don't know.
Yes, no, maybe?
If no, then who made me?
Who created the baby?
Oh, I just don't know.
**GOD**
Got the world on its knees.
Praying, begging, please.
Churches fill with folks.
Crosses promise hope.
Can so many be so wrong?
Was He here? Is He gone?
Made this place and then quit?
Took one look and just split?
**GOD**
What a con this could be.
A hip, slick tragedy.
Is it all just a myth?
Does He really exist?
Is She just total fiction?
A slick trick of some magician.
**I MEAN**
Where'd the sun come from,
And the moon and the stars?
Venus, cloudy blue,
And the red planet, Mars?
What about the mountains?
Who made the seas?
Check out the ice caps.
Who made them freeze?
**SURE**
Accidents can happen.
This wouldn't be the first.
But a sky whose high's forever
A never-ending universe?
**OH**
How I wish it was all great.
But it ain't.
There's earthquakes, tornadoes,
Tidal waves and hurricanes.
There's brains gone insane
And lungs that can't breathe.
Ears that can't hear
And eyes that can't see.
There's kids with no home.
Osteoporo-soft bones.
But for all the bad there's
twice as nice wonder.
Sunrise, sunset,
lightning, and thunder.
There's fires that fizzle.
Downpours that drizzle.
Solving a riddle and
Hearing a giggle
Of kids in the prime of their lives
Having the times of their lives.
**GOD?**
Oh, I don't know. At best it's a guess.
Ice cream, wet dreams, mashed potatoes with gravy.
Sweat-drenched sex. Oh, God?
Make. That. A
Yes.

**SHE'S** my heaven in a world of **HELL**
**SHE'S** the backbone to my **JELL**
**SHE'S** the aroma to my **SMELL**
**SHE'S** the secret I'll never **TELL**
**SHE'S** the body, breasts, and **BUTT**
**I'M** her squirrel, she's my **NUT**
**I'M** the bitter, she's the **SWEET**
**SHE'S** my faithful, I'm the **CHEAT**
**SHE'S** the rock that I **NEED**
**SHE'S** the band-aid when I **BLEED**
**SHE'S** my sister, she's my **MOTHER**
**SHE'S** my badass wild child **LOVER**
**SHE'S** my caution yellow **LIGHT**
**WARNIN'** me when shit ain't **RIGHT**
**SHE'S** the yes to my **MAYBE**
**SHE'S** the gift the good Lord gave **ME**
**SHE'S** the moonlight in the **DARK**
**SHE'S** the twinkle in the **STARS**
**I'M** the fuse, she's the **SPARK**
**SHE'S** my mini Noah's **ARK**
**SHE'S** the pillow on my **BED**
**SOFT**, safe place to lay my **HEAD**
**SHE'S** an angel in a world of **WITCH**
**BUT** make no **MISTAKE**
**SHE'S** still my **BITCH**

# The Way She Moves

It ain't the way she dances
Tippy-toe fancy prancin'
It ain't her education
Validicktory sensation
It's not about her logical rationale
Or keepin' secrets zip-lipped won't tell
Naaah

It's in The Way She Moves

Like a rotor motor turnin' over
When it's just been lubed

It's in The Way She Moves

Like a boa constrictor
Wraps around its victim
Straightening the noose

It's in The Way She Moves

Like a hammerhead cruisin'
Just beneath
the surface of the sea

It's in The Way She Moves

Like dynamite whose fuse is
'bout to blow my T.N.T.

She's the finest thing He ever created
Got the darkest, hardest skin, perfectly shaded
Got the Taj Mahal o' bodies
She's the hottest o' da hotties
She's Black Magic — dat's a fact
She's Black Magic — what an act
Magic and her pole done stole my soul and it be tragic
Damn dat Black Magic
Damn dat Black Magic

Got a face for Michaelangelo's last canvas
And a shape da Vinci hammered outta granite
She's de Milo wid two new arms
Wid Cleopatra's nasty-ass charms
She's Black Magic — dat's her name
She's Black Magic — she got game
Magic and her pole done stole my soul and ran me ragged
Damn dat Black Magic
Damn dat Black Magic

My mind be fantasizin' when she dances
She be groovin' body oozin' like molasses
She be grindin' she be floatin'
Like the ocean in slow motion
She's Black Magic — start to movin'
She's Black Magic — and I lose it
Magic and her pole done stole my soul, I done had it
Damn dat Black Magic
Damn dat Black Magic

I kin see it now
but I really can't
so I must admit
I just envision it

I mean

somewhere out there
deep in space
there's this creature
wid a face
that no one's ever
seen before
that's no one's ever
dreamed before

this chick who lives
in Galax City
who I ain't sure
you'd all call pretty
may factually be the girl
who's actually Ms. World

she's got three eyes
and the one in the back
got no brow
got no lash
but keeps her safe
from sneak attacks

the ones up front
are different too
the brown one and
the powder blue
tiny narrow sexy slits
that both transmit
"You can't come in"

dey ain't exactly
welcome mats
but that don't change the fact
you'll be back

'cause just one touch
o' dat skin
and just one look
at dat grin
screams of freak
and reeks from sin
dat will make you
face the fact
you'll be back

hair she wears
down to the ground
is thick and stiff
half black, half brown
'n' once they
find out about her
simply cannot
live without her

in the end,
my friends,
just trust
all y'all gonna fall
stone cold
in love with lust

anyone
can fantasize
dat don' come as
no surprise
but ya gotta
be slick or
sick-ass hip
to hit a chick
that thrives on lies
who's cold as ice
and hard as steel
makes love all night
but does not feel

c'mon, my friends,
don' be afraid
be strong, be brave
She's out there
you just might like
life as her slave
locked in chains

with more than
you ever wanted
and more than
you ever had
for once you
should forget being good
and hack-a-whack
at bad
yes, in the end, my friends
trust

all y'all's gonna fall

stone cold

in love with

lust

# She Be Out My League

Her father's from Great Britain (says he be's Royalty)
Her mum comes from Manhattan (but she acts like she is Queen)
But dis is 'bout the daughter dat they had
Da princess dat simply drives me mad
She's a sexy, smart freak
Got dat foreign intrigue
(Realistically speakin', she be out my league.)

Yeah she be out my league (pragmatically, it seems)
Except dat I done made the ghetto luv (star team!)
Yeah, she be out out my league (in yesterday's world)
But now I'm just another dude (and she be's just another girl)
Yes, one thing I done learned (from coming out da hood)
'S dat when it comes t' lovin', mine be's just as good.
No one is more special (no one's love be's better)
So I'm just gonna jump up (and go get her)
'Cause I done learnt one thing (from Mom and Dad)
Dat sometimes being good means being bad
She's part angel and she's part devil
A highbrow blueblood freak
She's somethin' extra special
But she be out my league

Yeah, she be out my league (if genes be all dat counts)
But lovin's all dat matters (when it comes to gettin' down)

Hotter than the sun, higher than the sky
Deeper than the ocean risin' at high tide
Other lovers love each other 24/7
Amen — for them — that's great
But me 'n' you need to get it 25/8
If ya got what we got, get it while it's hot
25/8

Frozen like the poles, solid like d' ice
Our bodies, hearts 'n' souls, stuck together for life
Some hearts drift apart 24/7
I guess — dat mess — is fate
But you 'n' me need to be — lovin'constantly — 25/8
When y' found what we done found y' gotta get down
25/8

Got a ninety-minute hour and a five-week month
A clock dat tick-tocks t' some down-home funk
Little stronger, little longer den 24/7
We just must perpetuate
No need for apprehension,
Just a bit of an extension 25/8
Y' won't regret it, gots t' get it
25/8

# Black Champagne

She ain't silk, she's mink
She ain't da flicker, she's da flame
She ain't Stoli or Jack, she's Black Champagne

She ain't gold, she's plat'num
Unbroken, untamed
Da stone-cold maximum, she's Black Champagne

She ain't sunset, she's the night
She ain't guilt, she's the blame
She's the meaning of life, she's Black Champagne

She's the epitome, infinity,
heads above the rest
Th' total truth, thousand-proof,
the absolute, the best

She ain't sunrise, she's high noon
She ain't game day, she's the game
She ain't moonlight, she's the moon, she's Black Champagne

She ain't famous, she be fame
She's Black Champagne
She's both picture and the frame
She's Black Champagne
She ain't comin', she done came
She's Black Champagne
She's the dollar arcade
She's Black Champagne
She's the soul Rose Bowl
She's Black Champagne

Hear ye, hear ye, all ye people
Da court says separate ain't equal
But you can't legislate equality
The racial problem's on you and me
Lincoln tried, but he done blew it
Emancipation Proclamation ain't do it
'Cause four hundred years can't be erased
There's too much pain, too much hate
Ain't no mo' plantations, ain't no mo' slaves
Some things are different but some ain't changed
There's life on the left and life on the right
There's life bein' black and life bein' white
There's polarization, mostly by choice
But somewhere out dere lives a sweet, soft voice

it's a drink in a bar
a wink of desire
a kiss in the dark
the start of a fire
it's a sigh in the night
of two bodies get down
it's black and white
creatin' new brown

Legislation can............drop dead and rot
Bodies can fix............what laws just cannot
Separation can't live............when love gets the hots
The problem'll be solved............deep down in
the crotch

# •E•P•I•T•O•M•E•

I believe there might be
Life on other planets
Where the females aren't
hardly as demandin'
Well, even if that's true
I have that here with you
'Cause you're the
other half of me
The love that makes
my life complete
A picture-perfect fit
for me
The absolute Epitome

I believe that there's a
queen of outer space
With an Einstein-fine mind
and gorgeous face
Whose kiss can melt lips with
just one taste
Well, even if she's real
Won't change how I feel
'Cause I created
you for me
You're my
home-grown fantasy
The absolute Epitome

You're high as I can fly
Hip as I can trip
My private positivity
My absolute Epitome

I believe there might be
Life in distant galaxies
Where super girls may
just be a reality
And monogamy is just
another fallacy
Well, even if that's right
It won't define my life
'Cause one'll be
enuff for me
You're the only
love I need
All there really is
of me
The absolute Epitome

You're the epitome of hot
The love I want non-stop
The epitome of sweet
The deepest of the deep
The epitome of smart
The blood that floods my heart
The epitome of funk
The funk that lets me dunk
The epitome of soul
Red hot and then ice cold
Everybody look 'n' see
I done found me the epitome
Look what God done made us be
The
Absolute
Epitome

# Asian Funk

[The inevitability of the preposterous!]

Asian Funk. Who woulda thunk it?
Who would think there'd be black pink?
Who woulda guessed 'bout B.T.S.
   Me, that's who. Let me hip you.
The universe should been diverse
   from the very first — but it wasn't,
   not when it comes to lovin'.
Ever since I been a kid
this ol' world done changed.
What used t' be is history.
Real been rearranged.
   White chicks be wid brothers.
   Sistas be wid whites.
   Or even wid each other.
   Ain' no wrong or right.
My dad would not believe it.
Mom'd have a stroke.
But to a dude like me,
finally there's hope
'cause I always envisioned
   colors living close
   — like, side by side.
My soul believed, passionately
   dat race should not divide.
I ain't positive that
opposites magically attract,
but I am damn sure
ain't no pure
   shades of white or black.
The only thing that's pure
   is an infant who's bran' new.
Black and white, like left and right
   are simply points of view.

Once upon tomorrow
everything will change.
Our brains'll all be smarter.
Our skins'll all be beige.
There'll just be one religion,
   piously devout.
God will be the dollar
   we cannot live without.
We'll each have us a rocket
   parked in our garage.
And sports craft built by NASA,
   distributed by Dodge.
Our kids will all be twins,
   identically the same.
They'll have to wear their name tags
   to differentiate.
Individuality will be misunderstood.
The Milky Way Galaxy
   Will be our neighborhood.
Love will be a lyric in some
   old romantic song.
We'll know it when we hear it,
   but the feeling won't last long.
Time flies when you're havin' funk.
   Brothers go to college.
White dudes dance and dunk and
   Rhythm's the new knowledge.

Yesterday's seeds — tomorrow's crops.
A world of weeds — wars nonstop.

Outer space is the next frontier.
More hatred, racism, pepperoni,
and Lite beer.

Asian Funk. Who woulda thunk it???

# I LOVE COLORED GIRLS

From Bermuda to Belize. Filipinos and Chinese.
Mexicanos, Sudanese. Prim and proper Japanese.
From Jamaica and San Juan. Smoking bodies, smoking guns.
Sweet Tahitians looking good. Sexy sisters from the hood.
Love Rihanna, Lucy Liu. Halle Barry, Carrie, too.
Native American Super Squaw. Colored ladies, I love 'em all.

Don't care where they're from.
Prejudice is dumb.
Color doesn't count
when you're gettin' down.

I love colored girls
Sexy textured colored girls
Red and black and yellow girls
for me
Lovers from around the world
for me

# Outro

REBEL
WITHOUT
APPLAUSE

I'm a rebel without applause
Don't no one clap for me
I'm a rebel without applause
They can't see what I see

I'm a rebel without applause
They don't hear me when I speak
I'm a rebel without applause
To them I'm just a freak

I'm a rebel without applause
Don't pat me on my back
I'm a rebel without applause
A sneaky, freak attack

Like Robert Kennedy said
Before he got shot dead
"I see a world that won't be stopped
"A peaceful world and ask 'Why not?'
"I see a country without states
"I see sex, but ain't no rape
"I see black and white together
"No one less than, no one better
"I see colors gettin' down
"Black and white becoming brown
"I see countries without borders
"I see free, fresh, clean, pure water
"I see cities without crime
"Where ain't nobody doing time"

I'm a rebel without applause
So don't write songs about me
I'm a rebel without applause
A mind that must fly free

I'm a rebel without applause
A voice that won't be stilled
I'm a rebel without applause
A dream that can't be killed

I'm a rebel without applause
No ovation yet for me
I'm a rebel without applause
A scout for what can be

I see earth as meant to be
All blue and green again
With air that's fit to breathe
Where progress and nature blend
I see a future when all men
From every continent
Are finally content
With one world government
I see black becoming beige
And yellow turning brown
I see racism erased
'Cause all y'all getting down
I see life from outer space
That just may pose a threat
I see earthlings as one race
That'll fight 'til our last breath

I'm a rebel without applause
Don't no one clap for me
I'm a rebel without applause
A scout for what can be

I'm a rebel without applause
A voice that won't be stilled
I'm a rebel without applause
A dream that can't be killed

I'm the devil's younger brother
The wicked witch's lover
When the status quo is gone
I'll be the reason and the cause
I'm a rebel, I'm a rebel
Without applause

# Color Blind

In this world of ours, Mother Nature made the flowers
red, yellow, violet, black, and white.
Flowers bloom together, people can do better
with Mother Nature helped by Father Time.
Mother Nature made lovers no special shade,
but she made you a special girl.
Mama made me, too, especially for you.
Together we can help to make this world color blind.

One day you will see, the whole wide world will be color blind.

Now, I come from my mother and even though I love her,
she told me that only white was right.
Then when I met you, I knew that wasn't true,
you gave a new meaning to my life.

Once upon a time, uneducated minds actually thought the world was flat.
Well, ignorance is wrong, hatred don't belong,
my other mother, Nature, taught me that.

One day you will see, the whole wide world gonna be color blind.

Clouds are white but they could be technically like you and me,
little puffs of love of boys and girls.
Black or white, what's the difference? All of us should just be living
side by side in this world.

There's a place for us, cuz in this world there's a place for all lovers.
And it's a warm, kind, wonderful place to be beside each other.
The whole wide world gonna be everyone living together as one.

In this world of ours, it's love that's got the power to be color blind.

She climbs in bed beside me
and kisses me on my cheek
"Get up, get up," she urges
**I act like I'm still asleep**

She climbs on like I'm a pony
and rides my eyes awake
Daylight starts dancin'
The bed begins to shake

**"Sleepyhead," she giggles**
ticklin' me as she rides
She laughs, whines, and wiggles
I open my eyes

I look up at Love
**She looks down at me**
That's how I get up
On weekends when I'm free

I don't need no buzzin'
or ringin' in my ears
**"I love you! I love you, Daddy,"**
is all I need to hear

Reveille's for soldiers
Alarm clocks are for fools
they're both a bad beginning
To days that are plain cruel

Dat pretty little lady's
my responsibility
The life how dat child lives
is solely up to me

So take away the trumpets
and disconnect the clock
The ringin' and the buzzin'
have simply got to stop

You took away my freedom
to feed your greed machine
But don't mess with my self-respect
or interrupt my dreams

Don't ring — don't buzz
I'll get up
I'll get up
**I'll get up for Love**

# Surprise-Surprise

**Surprise-Surprise** — I'm white and I'm hip
I love me some herb and some fine black chicks
**Surprise-Surprise** — I'm old and I'm bad
I hear all y'all, but I'm still my own man
I done been ev'rywhere 'round the world
Lived with and left all kinds of girls

I kin sing, rap 'n' roll right dere wid da brothers
Got a whole lotta soul 'n' I'm a badass lover
I kin think on my feet, improvise
I'm a funky ol' freak — **Surprise-Surprise**

**Surprise-Surprise** — I'm still a killa flirt
Got x-ray eyes and my johnson still works
**Surprise-Surprise** — I kin still get down
Love da ladies, black, white, yellow, red, and brown
Graduated college, master degreed
Top o' my class, Suma Cum Street
Hipped my kids to what da real deal was
That ev'ry color skin bleeds da same red blood
A hip from da wise should be sufficient enuff
Body, heart, and mind; life's all about love
I done lifted the rocks, uncovered the lies
Tell the truth, ain't ya shocked?
**Surprise-Surprise**

Oh, wow, I kin see things clearly now
Oh, yes, I'm finally at my best
My, my, my, what a wonderful surprise

**Surprise-Surprise** — I'm a badass dude
So don't come at me wid no lame attitude
Yeah, **Surprise-Surprise** — I may look past it
But so far, young bloods, y'all been outlasted
I done did a lotta stuff y' ain't did yet
Vegas laying odds y' just a 50/50 bet
So don' check me out and smack your lips
Young may be fun, but y' don' own hip
'Cause my heart kin still luv and my mind's still wise
Yeah I'm a human chameleon
**Surprise-Surprise**

Grey! How I dreaded the comin' o' da day
So I played me a hunch
Pumped up da funk
And let the brothers play the grey away
Age ain' just a number like ev'rbody says
It's trying t' pull you under, trying t' getcha dead
But ain' no way t' let it play
around wid your head
Gotta do what I done did
Pump da music up 'n' live
Gettin' down to da bass and da drums
Gettin' down ev'ry day keeps me young
I can run. I can jump. I can dunk.
I done found me Da Fountain o' Funk
Da Fountain o' Funk. Da Fountain o' Funk.
Ponce de Leon found it once
Followed me my hunch and found
Da Fountain o' Funk
When Meghan Trainor said it, she stated my case
Violins is pretty but it's all about da bass
Make love to the drummer
And turn da page on age
Gotta do what I done did
Pump da bottom up 'n' live
Listen to the rhythm flowing through your blood
Hold it in your soul, feel it in your guts
I found it. I found it. Da Fountain o' Funk
Da Fountain o' Funk. Da Fountain o' Funk.
The fountain o' youth was news once
Til I found Da Fountain o' Funk
Yeah. I found

I dreamt I dreamed a dream
seemed like a movie.
        A stereophonic, cinemascoptic, 3D, five-star doozy.
And da bitch dat did da castin'
picked a chick dat was fantastic as the lover of two brothers
wagin' war brother 'gainst brother —
rumblin' wid each other.
    And she be what they be fightin' for —
    once a young black slave that life locked up in chains.
    She grew to be knocked out fall down fine.
        Moved like black molasses — oozin' movin' past 'em —
            poked their souls and drove 'em out their minds.

Once da war was finished they had different opinions.
One said set her free — one was so opposed but both be simply schemin' —
secretly believin' dat da best bet was t' simply keep her close.
    Neither realized — though it was right before their eyes —
        that actually she despised 'em both.

        'Cause love don't grow enslaved
    and hearts locked up in chains
ain' 'bout to love the keeper wid the keys.
And if either one just watches and does nothin' to unlock it
Dey ain't never ever gonna get a piece.

Well — great movies lead to sequels
just like people lead to people.
        Generations pass and here we are.
Me, great grandson of rebel — devil number one —
And you, come from a slave became a star.
Well genes just keep repeatin' and like your predecedents
        Rhythm just believin' in your soul.

Even when you're standin' still
that thing inside you spills and
covers me wid funk dat's solid gold.

But when I look into your eyes I still see some despise
and realize dat da time ain't quite right yet.
A cent'ry's gone by but the pain of chains survives
'cause a brain once locked in chains cannot forget.

Yes — it seemed like a movie
A stereophonic, cinemascoptic, 3D, five-star doozy.
  But the thing is, in real life,
  it got shot in black and white.
  And the chick in da flick
  I wound up losin'

But dat stubborn streak in me
Will just shoot parts two and three
  — or four or more — long as there's a budget.
And even if I have to wait
  'til sequel number eight
somehow
  some day
    some way
      I pray you'll love me.

*Then I'll simply fade*
*the black and white t' beige*
*and share da happy ending*
*with the*
*public.*

the end of
"The End"

*and*
*The End*
*of*
*the book*

a project born of love and respect

PROS AND CONS
LEN BARRY
BLUEROOMBOOKS.COM

www.ingramcontent.com/pod-product-compliance
Lightning Source LLC
Chambersburg PA
CBHW040822050726
47507CB00021B/105
*9781950729067*